A Book of Wizards

A BOOK OF WIZARDS

Ruth Manning-Sanders

DRAWINGS BY

Robin Jacques

E. P. Dutton & Co., Inc.   New York

by the same author
and artist

A BOOK OF GIANTS

A BOOK OF DWARFS

A BOOK OF DRAGONS

A BOOK OF WITCHES

First published in the U.S.A. 1967 by E. P. Dutton & Co., Inc.
Copyright © 1966 by Ruth Manning-Sanders
All rights reserved. Printed in the U.S.A.

FIRST EDITION

Library of Congress Catalog Card Number: AC 67-10255

Foreword

Every country in the world has stories to tell about wizards. There are Red Indian wizards, and Chinese wizards, African wizards, English wizards, Celtic wizards, Greek, Italian, Arabian and Persian wizards. You will even find wizards in the Bible, where the Lord tells Moses that he 'shall stone them with stones'. That, of course, refers to the bad wizards; for, as there are good and bad witches, so there are good and bad wizards. But there are many more good wizards than there are good witches; for whereas a good witch is the exception, there seem to be just as many good wizards going about the world as bad ones.

The good wizards often go about disguised as poor old beggars, to test men's characters, and find out who has a kind heart and who a hard one. One such beggar-man-wizard you will find in the Hungarian story of *The Silver Penny*, another in the Tyrolean story *Gold*, and yet another in *Rich Woman, Poor Woman*, a story that comes from Flanders. And great are the rewards these beggar-men-wizards bestow upon those who are kind of heart; for wizards, on the whole, are even more powerful than witches.

In contrast with witches, also, many wizards have a sense of humour. They like to enjoy themselves; but witches always seem to be fierce and grim and very much in earnest. The wizard Auta, in the African story of *The Two Wizards*, is out for fun and nothing else. And in the Welsh story of *Jack and the Wizard*, one can almost hear the wizard chuckling to himself as he sets Jack his impossible-seeming tasks. 'Good, i' faith, good!' he says, every time Jack makes a success of things; he is really glad for Jack to succeed, and he probably knows quite well who is helping him. The whole thing seems to be just his little joke.

And now to take a look at the bad wizards. Perhaps the most famous of these is the wizard in the Arabian story, *Aladdin*. He is a real villain! And yet, despite his powerful magic, he is a somewhat foolish fellow, and after all his scheming he allows the princess to get the better of him.

In fact, these evil-minded wizards, clever as they may be, are never quite clever enough. Some little thing they overlook, and that little thing defeats them. In the Sicilian story of *Aniello*, the wizards are foiled by a mere mouse. In *Kojata*, a Russian story, the wizard has to go home because he can't pass a church (overlooking the fact that the church would disappear as soon as his back was turned). In the Italian story, *Cannetella*, the wizard is foiled by stumbling over a fallen door (he might just as well, one would think, have changed himself into an eagle and flown away with Cannetella). The Norse wizard, Farmer Weathersky, most foolishly lets himself get killed in the guise of a cock. And though, to be sure, in the story of *Long, Broad and Sharpsight*, which comes from Bohemia, the wizard nearly wins, yet he, too, has to admit defeat at the last moment. And this, of course, is all as it should be; because, as every fairy tale assures us, there is that in evil which brings about its own ruin; and in the fairy tale world, at any rate, wickedness never pays.

Contents

I · *Aniello*

You must know there was a lad called Aniello; and believe me, that lad was poor! He lived in a little hovel of a place, and he possessed nothing in the world but one little speckled hen. The little hen laid him an egg for his breakfast every morning, and that, at least, was something. But after a bit this hen got old and died. Aniello grieved about that: he was fond of his little hen; and besides – what was he to have for his breakfast now?

Said he to himself, 'I must take my poor little hen to market. Someone may perhaps give me a coin or two for her.'

So he went to market, and walked up and down, calling out, 'Who'll buy my little dead hen, who'll buy?'

But nobody seemed to want that little hen; so he sat down on the pavement with the hen across his knees. Then up came two wizards. Aniello didn't know they were wizards. They looked just like a couple of gypsies – but wizards they were.

Said one wizard, 'I'll give you half a ducat for that hen.'

Aniello was just going to say 'Done!' when somebody tweaked him by the sleeve. It was an old man, and the old man stooped and whispered in Aniello's ear, 'Don't have anything to do with those two men, my poor lad – they are wizards, and bad ones. The little speckled hen has a magic stone in her head. You have only to rub that stone and wish, and whatever you wish for will be yours.'

So then Aniello jumped up, tucked the little hen under his arm, and ran off home as fast as he could.

He took a knife and cut off the head of that little dead hen; and

9

sure enough in the top of her head he found a red stone. He rubbed the stone; and the very first thing he wished for was that his little speckled hen might come alive again and be able to speak to him.

No sooner wished than done. The little hen's head joined on to her body – she was a young hen now, not an old one. And she opened her yellow beak and said, 'Thank you, master.'

'Oh my dear little hen!' said Aniello. 'What shall I wish for next?'

'Something to eat for us both,' said the little hen.

So Aniello rubbed the red stone, and wished that wish – and there you were: a bowl full of corn appeared on the kitchen floor; the kitchen door opened, and in walked a table laid with a dish of meat, a dish of pudding, a loaf of bread, and a mug of beer.

Aniello and the little speckled hen ate till they were full; then the corn bowl and the table disappeared.

'Oh ho! my little hen,' said Aniello, 'now we shall live in clover! What shall we wish for next?'

The little speckled hen shut one eye; she scratched the side of her head with her little yellow claws, and thought. Then she said, 'Would you like to marry a princess?'

'I shouldn't mind,' said Aniello.

'Then wish for a grand castle with men servants and women servants to wait on you, and twenty fine horses in the stable and fine clothes for yourself, and a cellar full of money. Oh, and you might just as well wish to be the handsomest man in the world.'

Aniello rubbed the stone, wished all those things, and there you were: his hovel turned into a castle, with men servants and women servants, and twenty fine horses in the stables, and a cellar full of money; and he himself was sitting in a lordly room – as handsome a man as you could find if you searched the whole world through, and dressed like a lord, too. And the little speckled hen was perched on his knee.

'Oh ho, my little hen! What next?'

'A letter to the king to ask for his daughter,' said the little speckled hen. 'You write it, and I'll take it.'

So Aniello wrote a letter asking for the king's daughter in marriage, and the little speckled hen took the letter and hurried off with it to the palace. She found an open window and flew in through it; and she found the king, too – she was a clever little hen, and knew her way about. She stood before the king and made such a low bow that her beak touched the floor; then she lifted her head up high and said, 'My gracious sovereign, I bring you a letter from Lord Aniello.'

The king was so astonished that he nearly tumbled off his throne. 'What, you can *speak*!'

'Of course I can speak,' said the little speckled hen. 'My lord Aniello has given me a voice. My lord Aniello is a mighty lord – none mightier in the world. If you will look out of the window, you will see his castle over there, shining in the sun.'

The king looked out of the window – there was the castle shining in the sun. 'I did not know there was such a magnificent place in all my kingdom!' he said.

'My lord Aniello caused it to be built,' said the little speckled hen. 'He is so rich that he can buy and build what he pleases. He has a cellar full of gold, and a cellar full of silver, and a cellar full of precious stones.'

'I would like to meet this Lord Aniello!' said the king. 'But let me read his letter and see what he desires of me.'

When the king read the letter and understood that Aniello wished to marry his daughter, he was delighted. He summoned the princess to him and said, 'My girl, your fortune is made! The richest lord in the world is asking for your hand in marriage.'

'But is he young and handsome?' said the princess.

The king hadn't thought about that. '*Is* he young and handsome?' he said to the little speckled hen.

'Send for him and you will see,' said the little speckled hen.

So the king sent for Aniello, and Aniello came. The princess looked him up and down, and thought 'Yes'; the king looked him up and down, and thought 'Most certainly'. And Aniello and the princess were married as soon as the king could possibly manage it.

For some time they were happy. The princess was rather spoilt and rather vain, and she wanted her own way in most things. But then, Aniello had only to rub the red stone and wish, and he could give her everything she asked for, whether clothes or jewels, or little dogs, or horses to ride on, or elegant carriages to drive her about. She didn't care much for Aniello, certainly; but she cared much for what he gave her. And as to Aniello, he was a simple fellow and liked her well enough, though he liked his little speckled hen better.

But what about those two wizards? Were they going to leave Aniello in peace with his magic stone? Not if they knew it! They wanted that stone for themselves, and they meant to have it. So they made a little doll, the prettiest little doll in the world. The doll had three buttons in its back: if you pressed the first button, it would get up and dance; if you pressed the second button, it would curtsy and say, 'Good morning, mama, I hope you are well this morning?' And if you pressed the third button, it would open its rosebud of a mouth very wide, and sing, 'Oh dear me, what a flower I be!'

When they had made this doll, the wizards disguised themselves as gypsies and went to Aniello's castle at an hour when they knew Aniello would not be there, for it was the king's custom to summon Aniello over to the palace every morning.

The king had come to rely on Aniello more and more. It seemed to the king that whatever problems or troubles he had, Aniello would be sure to put things right for him. And this was true, because Aniello kept the red stone in his pocket, and when the king began to fuss and fume and complain of everything going wrong, Aniello would put his hand in his pocket, rub the stone and wish, 'May everything go right for the king.' And at once everything did go right.

Well, the two wizards, in their gypsy dresses, went to the castle, sat down in the courtyard, placed the little doll on the ground, and put her through her tricks. You may be sure they soon had a delighted crowd of spectators gathered round them!

The princess was sitting at a window, yawning. She was bored, waiting impatiently for Aniello to come home, and wondering

13

what next she could ask him to give her. He seemed to have given her everything, but everything was not enough.

'Oh, how dull life is!' she thought. 'Why doesn't something happen?'

She called one of her ladies to sing to her – she slapped the poor lady because she sang a note out of tune. She called another of her ladies to read to her, and slapped *her* because she mispronounced a word. Then she looked into the courtyard.

'What is all that crowd doing down there?' she asked yet another of her ladies. 'Go and see.'

The lady ran off, and came back smiling. 'Oh my princess,' she said, 'there are two gypsies with a marvellous doll – it can dance and sing and talk!'

At last! Here was something interesting! 'Bid them bring the doll up to me,' said the princess.

The wizards brought up the doll, and set it on the floor. First it danced, and then it curtsied and said, 'Good morning, mama, I hope you are well this morning?' And then it opened its rosebud of a mouth wide, wide, wide, and sang, 'Oh dear me, what a flower I be!'

The princess was delighted. She said she would buy the doll; but the wizards told her it was not for sale.

'But I must have it!' cried the princess.

'My princess,' said one of the wizards, 'though the doll is not for sale, we shall be honoured to give it to you —'

'In return for a trifling favour,' said the other wizard.

'Any favour! Name your favour!' cried the princess.

'My lord Aniello possesses a red stone,' said the first wizard. 'It is of no value, but our mother, who is the queen of the gypsies, had one like it set in a ring which she has lost.'

'And if we might borrow my lord Aniello's red stone – just for an hour or two – we would have it copied and set in a ring to give to our mother,' said the other wizard.

The princess immediately sent off a page to the palace with a note to Aniello. The note said, 'Best beloved husband, please lend me your red stone for an hour.'

Aniello, foolish fellow, thinking no evil, gave the stone to the page; the page took it to the princess; the princess gave it to the wizards, and got the doll. And the wizards went off with the stone.

'Ha! Ha! Ha!' laughed one wizard. And 'Ho! Ho! Ho!' laughed the other wizard. 'Aniello will never see his red stone again!'

They hastened away to a forest outside the town. They threw off their gypsy disguise. One rubbed the stone and said, 'May the stone lay waste all that it has done!' The other rubbed the stone and said, 'May the stone carry us far, far away!'

No sooner wished than done. The wizards vanished. Aniello's castle melted away, the princess found herself in the kitchen of Aniello's old hovel; and Aniello, who was standing in the council chamber with the king, listening to his grievances, turned into his former self.

The king glared at Aniello: he did not know him. Aniello was dressed in rags, and his face was the rough, sun-tanned face of a peasant.

'What are you doing here?' cried the king in a rage. 'How dare you come into my presence? Be off with you!'

'My gracious king – ' began Aniello.

'Be off, I say!' cried the king. 'Turn him out, somebody! Where is my lord Aniello? Find him, somebody!'

The courtiers hustled Aniello from the council chamber; they ran him downstairs to the porter, and the porter kicked him out through a side door.

The king was still calling for Aniello; they sought him high and low, but of course they couldn't find him. For the poor ragged peasant lad that was Aniello had tumbled down in the dust of the courtyard.

Aniello picked himself up and set off for his castle. Where *was* his castle? It had gone, and there in its place was his old hovel. He pushed open the door of his hovel and went in. In the kitchen, the princess was sitting on a wooden stool.

'My stone!' cried Aniello. 'Quick, give me my stone!'

'*Your* stone!' said the princess. 'Who are *you*?'

'I am Aniello – give me my stone, and you will see!'

The princess began to scream. 'You are *not* Aniello, and I haven't got the stone. I lent it to the gypsies.'

Then Aniello remembered the gypsies who had wanted to buy his little dead hen, and he cried out, 'Oh my red stone, oh my poor little hen, oh my wicked wife – you have undone me, my wicked wife!'

'I am *not* your wife, you dirty peasant!' screamed the princess. And she ran out of the hovel and went back to her father's palace.

Aniello looked down at his clothes: they were rags. He looked at his face in a cracked mirror: it was a good honest face, but nobody could call it the handsomest face in the world. He laid his arms on the table, and his head on his arms, and wept.

Then he heard his little hen clucking: he looked up – there she was, perched on the table. She had changed from a young hen back into an old one. Aniello stretched out his hand and stroked her head. 'Oh my little hen, tell me what I am to do!'

'*Cluck, cluck!*' said the little hen. Alas! it was all she could say! Then she flew down from the table and went to the door.

'*Cluck-cluck!*' she said again, and fluttered her wings.

'I know, I know!' said Aniello. 'I know what you are telling me. We will set out and search through the world; we will never cease from searching until we find the wizards and get back our stone!'

'*Tuc-a-tuc-taw!*' said the little hen.

So Aniello took a stout staff in his hand, put a loaf of bread in a knapsack, slung the knapsack over his shoulder, tucked the little hen under his arm, and set out.

He went, and he went, and he went, asking everyone he met if they had seen anything of two gypsies. But nobody had. When the loaf of bread was eaten, he had to beg his way, but still he went. He went through all the kingdoms of the world, he passed through the kingdom of the cats, and came to the kingdom of the mice.

The mouse army seized him and took him to their king; they thought he was a spy sent by the cats. Aniello told his story to the mouse king, and the mouse king said, 'I see you have been most unfairly treated, and if I can help you, I will.' Then he blew a whistle to summon all the mouse elders to a grand council.

However, none of the mice could think of any way to help Aniello.

'But are we all here?' said the mouse king. 'I think one of our number is missing.'

Then the little hen looked towards the door of the council chamber. '*Tuc, tuc!*' she said. The door opened, and in came an old, old mouse, quite grey with age, hobbling slowly on his little stiff legs.

'You are late!' said the mouse king. 'It does not please me that any of my councillors should not arrive in time. Are you gone deaf with age that you did not hear my summons?'

The little grey mouse stood up on his little stiff hind legs, and said, 'Oh my king, a thousand pardons! I heard your summons, but I was far, far away, in the castle of Rampino, which stands on the edge of the world.'

'And what were you doing there?' said the king.

'I was learning of the wickedness that exists on earth,' said the old grey mouse. 'Such wickedness as you, my king, have never dreamed of. I heard two wizards boasting of how they had stolen a red stone, and ruined the happiness of a good lad called Aniello.'

Aniello shouted, the little hen clucked, the councillors cheered; the mouse king clapped his paws together and cried, '*Silence!*'

Then you could have heard a pin drop, and the king said, 'This is Aniello. Take him to the castle of Rampino.'

17

So Aniello and the little hen and the old grey mouse set out for the castle of Rampino on the edge of the world; and long and long was the time it took them to get there. A river flowed by the castle, and trees grew by the river.

'We will sit down here under the trees and take our rest,' said the old grey mouse. 'And when night comes and the wizards are asleep, I will go into the castle and see if I can find the red stone.'

So they all sat and rested until night.

Then the old grey mouse went into the castle, and crept and crept, upstairs and along corridors, until he came to the wizards' bedroom. They were both asleep; one of them had his hand resting on the coverlet; and on a finger of that hand was a ring with the red stone in it.

The old grey mouse climbed up on to the bed, and began to gnaw at the wizard's finger. If he had to gnaw the finger right off, he would get that ring! But the wizard, feeling the pain, stirred in his sleep and mumbled, 'Bah! how this ring hurts!' And he took it off his finger and laid it on a table by the bed.

And the old grey mouse took the ring in his mouth and ran off with it to Aniello.

Aniello put the ring on his finger and rubbed the stone. And the very first thing he wished for was that his little hen might become young again and be able to speak to him.

No sooner wished than done! There was the little old hen turned young again; and she opened her yellow beak and said, 'Thank you, master!'

'Oh my dear little hen,' said Aniello, 'what shall I wish for next?'

The little hen cocked her head towards the old grey mouse and said, 'Ask *him*.'

So Aniello said to the old grey mouse, 'And you, would you like to become young again?'

And the old grey mouse answered, 'Thank you, sir, but wisdom comes with age. I prefer to remain as I am.'

Then Aniello rubbed the stone, and wished that the wizards might be turned into asses; and the castle gates opened and out they came, two asses, braying and shaking their long ears, and looking very foolish.

'So!' said Aniello, and rubbed the stone yet again. 'I wish that one of you may be loaded with cheese and salt pork.'

Immediately two panniers fell from the clouds on to the back of the nearest ass: one pannier loaded with cheese, and the other with salt pork.

Then Aniello put the old grey mouse in his pocket, and tucked the little hen under his arm, took the loaded ass by the halter, jumped on to the back of the other ass, and rode off to the kingdom of the mice.

And on the way he said, 'Oh my dear little hen, what shall I wish for next?'

'Well, you might wish to be the handsomest man in the world again,' said the little speckled hen.

No sooner wished than done. There was Aniello now, as handsome a man as you could find though you searched the whole world through. And he rode on merrily to the kingdom of the mice.

There he took the old grey mouse from his pocket and set him down before the king. Then he presented the king with the cheese and salt pork. The mice sat down and feasted; and when they could eat no more, they swarmed about the two asses and ran up their legs and bit them, and drove them away into the wilderness. And in the wilderness they have remained from that day to this.

Said Aniello to the little speckled hen, 'My good little hen, what shall I wish for now?'

'I think you might wish to be dressed in fine clothes and back in your castle.'

Aniello rubbed the stone and wished that wish. He had scarcely said good-bye to the mouse king and thanked him, than he was back in his castle, sitting in a lordly room and dressed like a lord, and with the little speckled hen perched on his knee.

Everything was right now, except one thing. Aniello did not want his wife back. He thought and thought about this, and he grew sad.

Said the little speckled hen, 'Master, why are you sad?'

'Oh, my little hen,' said Aniello, 'I have a vain, selfish, deceitful wife. I should be happier without her.'

'Then wish her married to somebody else,' said the little hen.

Aniello rubbed the stone and wished that wish.

'Now send a page to the king's palace for news,' said the little speckled hen.

Aniello sent the page for news. The page came back and said that the king was giving a wedding feast. He had cancelled the princess's first marriage, and she was wedded to the King of Tartary.

'So now you are happy, Master?' said the little hen.

Aniello was rubbing his hands together in a thoughtful kind of way. 'Yes,' he said, 'I suppose I am happy. But oh, my dear little hen, I owe all my happiness to you, and you are more precious to me than anything else in the world. I wish you were a maiden that I might marry you!'

He didn't know that he was rubbing the red stone, but he was. And, hey presto! the little speckled hen disappeared, and there in her place stood a beautiful maiden.

The maiden dropped Aniello a curtsey. 'Master, your little speckled hen thanks you for disenchanting her!'

Aniello took her in his arms. 'We will be married this very day!' he cried.

And so they were.

After they were married Aniello gave the red stone to his wife, and said, 'You are wiser than I am – the stone is safer with you.'

So Aniello's wife kept the stone. She did much good with it, and made many people happy; but none happier than herself and Aniello.

2 · The Two Wizards

There were once three brothers who lived together in a pleasant house. The brothers had money; there was no need for them to work, so the two elder spent their time playing draughts. But the youngest – Auta was his name – studied magic day and night. He became a wizard. Then he changed himself into a horse and said, 'Brothers, plait a rope and a hobble, lead me into the city and sell me.'

The brothers plaited a rope and a hobble. They led the horse into the city. He was a beauty! The king bought him, and paid twelve elephants for him.

The two brothers went home with the elephants. The king got on the horse to ride him. The horse went prancing, prancing, prancing. The king said, 'Well! Never in my life have I met with such an enjoyable horse!' And he rode the horse to his palace.

At the gates of the palace the king dismounted. What did the horse do then? He bolted.

The king cried out, 'Catch that horse! Catch him! Catch him!' The king's servants ran to the stables, they led out horses, they jumped on their backs, they set off in pursuit. Could they overtake the horse that was Auta? They could not. He out-galloped them all.

But the king had a wizard of his own, whom he kept to advise him. And the king's wizard said, 'Set one wizard to catch another!' And he, too, changed himself into a horse, and set off galloping.

The horse that was Auta was now grazing in a meadow. He pricked up his ears. He heard the sound of galloping. The horse that was the king's wizard came charging across the meadow. The horse that was Auta changed himself into a white eagle, and flew up into the sky. The horse that was the king's wizard changed himself into a black eagle and flew up after the white one. The white eagle changed himself into a hawk, and flew down among the trees. The black eagle changed himself into a kite, and flew down after the hawk. Under the trees Auta's two brothers sat playing draughts. The hawk changed himself into a draught and fell down on the board.

The kite changed himself into a man. He said to the brothers, 'Give me my draught!'

The brothers said, 'All these draughts are ours!'

The man said, 'Count the pieces.'

The brothers counted the pieces – one too many!

They said, 'Well, take it!'

The man put out his hand to take the draught. It turned into a scorpion.

The man changed himself into a striped snake: he was going to swallow the scorpion.

But the scorpion changed himself into a speckled snake, too large to be swallowed.

The snakes coiled themselves on their tails and looked at each other. Neither could swallow the other.

Then the speckled snake said, 'Here, let us arise and become men!'

They arose, they became men. Auta and the king's wizard stood looking at each other.

Auta said, 'Is it because of the twelve elephants that you have pursued me?'

The king's wizard said, 'Well, I live with the king. I am his wizard. Now shall another wizard come and steal his property? If I were to allow that, I should be a traitor.'

Auta said, 'It was all a joke. I will send the elephants back to the king. Now you can go home.'

The king's wizard said, 'How can I go home? I don't know the way from here.'

Auta said, 'We will change ourselves into crows, and I will lead you back to the king's city.'

So they changed themselves into crows. Auta flew before, and the king's wizard flew behind. And they came in sight of the king's city.

Auta said, 'You will find the elephants have returned. Now good-bye.'

So one crow flew away, and the other crow changed himself into the king's wizard, and went into the city.

The king said to his wizard, 'Did you catch that horse?'

The king's wizard said, 'No, I didn't. I followed him and followed him for three days, but I couldn't catch him.'

The king said, 'Never mind. I don't want the horse. It was unmanageable. And the elephants have come back. But here is a present for your trouble.'

And the king gave his wizard a million cowries.

Auta had gone home laughing. His brothers didn't know what to make of him. They went on playing draughts. And Auta went on studying magic day and night.

3 · Long, Broad and Sharpsight

There was a king who was a widower, and he had but one son. When the prince was grown up the king said to him, 'My son, it is time you married.'

The prince said, 'My father, I would gladly marry, but where shall I find a bride?'

The king took a golden key from his pocket and gave it to the prince. 'Go, climb to the top of the eastern tower,' he said. 'Unlock that which is locked, and enter. It may be that you will find something to your fancy.'

The prince took the golden key and went to the eastern tower. He did not know what was up there – nobody knew, for nobody ever went there. It was full of cobwebs. There was a winding stair, and the prince climbed up and up till he could go no farther. Above him now was a low ceiling, and in the ceiling was a locked iron door. The prince reached and unlocked the door with the golden key, pushed the door back, and swung himself up.

Now he was in a large circular room. The ceiling of the room was blue, like the sky on a clear night, and it glittered with silver stars. On the floor was a carpet of green silk, and round the room were twelve high windows in golden frames. Eleven of the windows were of stained glass, glowing with colour; and on each of them was a picture of a beautiful maiden, wearing a crown on her head.

But the twelfth window was covered with a white curtain.

The prince looked from the picture of one maiden to the picture of another maiden. He was astonished at their beauty. He gazed and gazed: he could not tell which was the most beautiful. And as he looked at those maidens, they began to move and smile. One held out her hands to him as if to say, 'Let me be your bride – choose me!' And another held out her hands to him as if to say, 'No, choose me!'

Long and long he gazed at them. And still he could not decide which one he would rather have for his bride; for they were all as lovely as the dawn.

And so, moving from window to window, he came to stand before the one that was covered by a white curtain. He drew back the curtain to see what was behind it.

'O-o-oh! . . .' A maiden in a white dress, girt with a silver girdle, and wearing a crown of pearls – a sad, pale maiden, who neither held out her hands to him, nor smiled, but only gazed at him with eyes that were big with sorrow. The look in those sorrowful eyes struck the prince to the heart. He knelt before the picture, held out his hands to the maiden, and cried, 'It is you I will have for my bride, and none other!'

Then all the pictures disappeared; and the prince was standing in a room without a single window.

He ran down from the tower and went to the king. 'My father,' he said, 'I have chosen my bride! It is the maiden behind the curtained window.'

'Oh my son, my son,' cried the king, 'what have you done? Surely you have brought great trouble upon yourself! Was there not choice enough among the eleven maidens, but you must needs unveil that which was better veiled? This maiden is in the power of a wicked wizard, and is kept prisoner in an iron castle. Many brave lads have set out to free her, but of those brave lads not one has returned to tell the tale. Put her from your mind, my son; go up into the tower again and choose another bride. Surely out of the eleven maidens you can find one beautiful enough to please you!'

'They are all beautiful,' said the prince. 'Their beauty spoke to my eyes and troubled my mind. But the beauty of the sorrowful maiden spoke to my heart, and I will have no other bride.'

Seeing that the prince was determined, the king gave him a good horse and a purse full of money, and bade him go seek his bride. 'I cannot tell you which way you must go,' he said, 'for I do not know it. I can only give you my blessing and pray for your safe return.'

The prince knelt to receive his father's blessing. Then he set out. He travelled for many days. He came at last into a dense forest, and there he lost the road. He wandered with his horse through tangled thickets, over deep morasses, and among huge rocks. He could find no way forward, and no way back.

Then he heard a shout behind him: 'Stop, prince, stop!'

The prince looked round. There, hurrying after him, was a very tall man.

'My name is Long,' said the very tall man. 'If you will take me into your service, you will never regret it, for I can do what other people cannot do. Look up! Do you see a bird's nest on the top of that pine? I will bring that nest down to you without having to climb.'

'How can you do that?'

'Wait and you will see.'

Long began stretching himself. He stretched himself and stretched himself until he was as tall as the pine. He picked up the bird's nest, he shrank again, and handed the nest to the prince.

'But the nest is no use to me,' said the prince. 'And the mother bird will be sorrowful. Put it back. You would be of more use if you could show me the way out of this wood.'

'That I can easily do!' said Long. He stretched himself to the height of the pine, and put the nest back on its branch. But now he did not shrink again; he went on stretching and stretching until he was three times as tall as the tallest tree in the forest. And then he turned his head this way and that on his long neck.

'I see the way we must go!' he called. And he shrank down again, took the prince's horse by the bridle, and led it forward.

In less than no time they were out of the forest.

Before them now was an immense plain. Beyond the plain were huge grey rocks, packed so closely together that they looked like the walls of a great city. And beyond the grey rocks towered mountains, with clouds on their shoulders and snow on their tops.

Long looked across the plain. 'My prince, I see a friend of mine. If you would take him also into your service, you would not regret it.'

The prince said, 'Call him to me.'

Long said, 'He is too far off to hear my call. I will fetch him.'

Then Long stretched himself out to such a height that his head vanished in the clouds. He made a bow of his body and reached out his arms over the plain. He picked up his friend and set him down at the side of the prince's horse.

This friend was a short, fat little fellow with a round, smiling face. He was almost as wide as he was high.

The prince looked at him. 'Who are you?' he said. 'And what can you do?'

'My name is Broad, sir. I can widen myself.'

'Show me.'

'But back into the forest first,' cried Broad. 'Back for your life!'

The prince didn't see why he should go back into the forest. But Long seized the horse's bridle and took a stride – and there was the prince, willy nilly, galloping away among the trees. Just as well, or prince and horse would have been squashed to jelly; for Broad was swelling and swelling in all directions. He swelled till his body covered everything everywhere, just as if a mountain had rolled up.

'Enough, enough!' called Long, who was watching him from over the top of the forest trees. So then Broad took himself in again, and the draught of his shrinking was so great that all the trees in the forest roared and swayed as if in a mighty storm.

The prince and Long came out of the forest. 'I would rather have you as a friend than an enemy!' said the prince to Broad. And he took Broad into his service.

The three of them journeyed on across the plain; and when they drew near the barrier of huge grey rocks, they met a man who had his eyes bandaged with a handkerchief.

Said the man, 'Will you take me into your service, my prince?'

Said the prince, 'You are welcome to travel along with us. But I do not think that a blind man can be of much service to me.'

'Blind!' cried he of the bandaged eyes. 'I am not blind! I see only too clearly. With my bandaged eyes I see you as clearly as you see me. If I unbandage my eyes I look through everything. And when I look sharply at anything it catches fire and bursts into flame, or if it cannot burn, it splits to pieces. That is why I am called Sharpsight. You see this wall of rock?'

'Yes,' said the prince, 'I see it well enough, and it bars our way.'

'Not it!' said Sharpsight. He snatched the bandage from his eyes and looked fixedly at the tightly packed rocks. On the instant the rocks began to crackle. They smoked, they split, they fell to pieces; nothing was left of them but a heap of sand.

'Sharpsight, I will indeed take you into my service!' said the prince. 'But come, look about you. Tell me, do you anywhere see an iron castle?'

Sharpsight looked about him. He looked east, he looked west, he looked south. Then he looked north and cried, 'I see it! And I see *into* it!'

'Do you see my princess?'

'I see her weeping, weeping, behind an iron lattice in a high tower,' said Sharpsight.

'Then let us hasten to her rescue!' cried the prince.

And they all set off towards the north.

It was a long, long way. Perhaps they never would have reached that iron castle had not Long stretched himself out and lifted them each in turn over the heaps of sand, up over the great mountains, and down on the other side. But there was the iron castle at last, standing on a desolate heath.

The sun was setting behind them, the castle glowed red in its rays, and they saw that it was surrounded by a deep moat, crossed by an iron bridge. They went over the iron bridge, and through iron gates into the castle courtyard. And scarcely had they got into the courtyard than the sun went down below the horizon. The iron bridge swung up, the iron gates clanged shut. And there they were, all four of them, prisoners!

'But I can easily lift you all out again,' said Long.

'No, no!' said the prince. 'I would rather be inside than outside, since my princess is here. But I see a stable yonder. Take my horse, Long, and if there is food in the stable, feed him well.'

Long led the horse to the stable, and soon came back. 'There is plenty of fodder there,' he said, 'and there are plenty of horses, too. But they will make poor company, for they are all turned to stone.'

'And my horse?' said the prince anxiously.

'Alive and well,' said Long, 'and eating his head off.'

'Then let us go into the castle,' said the prince, 'for I see the doors are open.'

They went in. What did they see? Crowds of people everywhere – in the halls, in the corridors, in every room. But none of those people moved or spoke: they were all turned to stone.

'Oh my princess, my princess!' thought the prince. 'Is this to be my fate too?'

They walked on, the prince and his three comrades, from room to room. They saw stone princes with their swords raised, as if

about to strike. They saw stone knights with their heads turned over their shoulders, stumbling forward as if in flight. By a stone fire they saw a stone cook standing over a cauldron with a ladle in his hand; and in the chimney corner they saw a stone servant. In one hand he held a plate of meat; with the other hand he was raising a slice of meat to his mouth – and all was stone.

At last they came into a brightly lit hall in which there were no stone figures; but there was a table laid for four people. There was meat and wine and fruit and bread on the table, and as they were all very hungry, they sat down and ate.

They had scarcely finished their meal when the door of the hall flew open, and two people came in. One was the wizard himself: a bent old man with a bald head and a long grey beard. He was dressed in a black robe, tightly girdled about with three iron hoops; and he led by the hand a maiden whiter than snow, wearing a white robe with a silver girdle, and with a crown of pearls on her head.

The prince leaped to his feet. 'My princess!' he cried.

The wizard grinned most evilly. 'Is she your princess, *is* she?' he mocked. 'Not so fast, young man! You have come to fetch her away, have you? Well, well, take her if you can! But first you must keep her in sight for three nights. And if you can't keep her in sight, if she vanishes from you, you will be turned into stone like all these other fools! See, now she shall sit at table with you, and I wish you all a very good evening!'

The wizard then burst into shrieks of laughter and went away. The princess sat at the table. She looked sad, oh so sad! The prince talked and talked to her; he told her of his love, of how he had come to set her free. He besought her to say one word to him. But the princess neither spoke nor smiled. Her great eyes were full of sorrow, and her face was deadly pale.

'I will not stir from your side!' cried the prince. 'I will not close my eyes! I will keep watch all night – you shall not vanish from me!'

'*I* will make sure that she does not go out of the room!' said Long. And he stretched himself out like a strap, and wound himself round the whole room along the walls. Broad stood in the doorway and swelled himself out, till not a crack of the door was left unfilled – not even the tiniest fly could have got in or out of that door. And Sharpsight posted himself against a pillar in the middle of the hall, watching on all sides.

But at midnight a little warm breeze came stealing through the hall. The little warm breeze blew into the face of the the prince, and into the faces of Long and Broad and Sharpsight; and immediately there they were, all fast asleep.

And the little warm breeze lifted up the princess and carried her away.

The prince woke at the first streak of dawn. He yawned, stretched himself, looked round – there was no princess!

'Wake! Wake! Wake!' he shouted to his three comrades. 'The princess has gone!'

They all woke. Sharpsight snatched the bandage from his eyes. He looked, with his piercing sight, far far away. 'I see her!' he cried. 'A hundred miles from here there is a wood; in the wood there is an oak tree; on the oak tree is an acorn. The princess is that acorn. Come, comrade Long, take me on your shoulders!'

Long took Sharpsight on his shoulders. He stretched himself and stretched himself. He strode twenty miles with each step, and Sharpsight showed him the way. He reached the wood, he plucked the acorn from the oak. In ten seconds he was there and back again, and handing the acorn to the prince.

'My prince, let it fall on the ground.'

The prince let the acorn fall to the ground. The acorn vanished: the princess stood before him.

Then the sun looked over the mountains; the door flew open

with a mighty crash, and the wizard bounced into the room. He was grinning horribly; but when he saw the princess his face grew purple with rage, and one of the iron hoops which girdled his waist burst with a bang. He seized the princess by the hand, and led her away.

Breakfast appeared on the table, and the prince and his comrades sat down to eat. They were not happy; they could not understand how they had all fallen asleep.

The prince went out to the stable; there, among the rows of stone horses, he found his own horse alive and well. The courtyard gates were wide open, and the iron bridge was spanning the moat. The prince took his horse out for a canter; but everything around him was desolate and dead. There were trees without leaves, there were meadows without grass, there was a river but it did not flow, there were no flowers, there were no birds. The prince went back into the iron castle and wandered about, looking at the stone figures.

At noon the four comrades sat down to another meal. The food appeared of itself on the table, the wine poured itself out. At sunset the iron bridge over the moat lifted itself up, and the courtyard gates clanged shut. Supper appeared on the table; the comrades ate again. They had scarcely finished their meal when the door of the hall flew open. The wizard, grinning horribly, led in the princess, and went out again.

'We will keep better watch tonight!' said the prince.

But at midnight came the warm breeze, forcing sleep upon them. And the breeze lifted the princess and carried her away.

At dawn the prince woke and gazed wildly round him.

'Sharpsight! Sharpsight!' he shouted. 'Wake! Wake! Wake! Where is the princess?'

Sharpsight looked with his piercing eyes. 'I see her!' he cried. 'Two hundred miles from here there is a mountain, and in the mountain a rock, and in the rock a precious stone. The princess is that stone. Come, Long, take me on your shoulders. Let us away!'

Long took Sharpsight on his shoulders and strode off. Twenty miles he went at each step. They reached the mountain. Sharpsight looked fixedly at it. His eyes blazed, the mountain crumbled, the rock split into a thousand pieces, and the precious stone glittered on the ground.

Sharpsight picked up the stone. Long lifted him on to his shoulders and strode off again. Twenty miles he went at each step, and in ten seconds they were back at the iron castle.

Sharpsight gave the precious stone to the prince; the prince dropped it on the ground; the stone vanished – there stood the princess.

The rising sun looked over the mountain tops; the door of the hall flew open, and in bounced the wizard. When he saw the princess he screamed with rage, and *bang!* a second iron hoop burst from around his waist. He took the princess by the hand, and led her away.

In the evening he brought the princess once more. 'You think yourself clever!' he said to the prince. 'But tonight we shall see who will win – you or I!' And he went out again.

'Tonight we *will* not sleep!' said the prince. 'We will not even sit down. We will walk about till dawn!'

They walked about, and they walked about till midnight.

Then came the little warm breeze, blowing through the hall. And even as they walked, they fell asleep and dropped to the ground.

And the little warm breeze lifted up the princess and carried her away.

The prince woke at dawn. 'Sharpsight, Sharpsight!' he shouted. 'The princess has gone!'

Sharpsight looked and looked. He looked here, he looked there. 'Oh my prince,' he cried at last, 'I see her, but she is very far off. Three hundred miles from here there is a black sea, and on the bottom, in the midst of the sea, lies a little shell. In the shell is a ring: the princess is that ring. But come, we may reach her in time, and today we must take Broad with us.'

Long took Sharpsight up on one shoulder, and Broad up on the other shoulder. He strode off – thirty miles at a stride. When they came to the black sea, Sharpsight said, 'Long, stretch out your arm to the midst of the sea. Then put down your hand and see if you can feel the shell.'

Long stretched out his arm to the midst of the sea. He put down his hand into the water; he groped and groped, but the shell was so small, he could not find it.

'Now it's my turn!' cried Broad.

He swelled himself up as far as his paunch would reach. He lay down on the shore and began to drink up the water. At every gulp the sea fell lower. In less than no time there was nothing left but a bed of black sand; and in the midst of the bed of black sand shone a small white shell. Long stretched himself out and picked up the shell. He opened it, took out the gold ring, lifted Sharpsight on to one shoulder, and Broad on to the other, and set off back for the iron castle.

But Broad, being full of black sea water, was huge and heavy. Long did his best to hurry; but Broad swayed and swung on his shoulder like an enormous sack. Long staggered on; he took an extra big stride, Broad toppled sideways – *thump!* he fell from Long's shoulder like a sack let fall from a tower. In a moment the valley through which they were passing was under water, like a vast lake. Poor Broad would have been drowned, had not Long snatched him up again.

Meanwhile, back in the iron castle, the prince was walking restlessly up and down the hall. Would his comrades never come back? Oh what was keeping them? The dawn was brightening; from behind the mountains the rising sun sent glimmering beams up into the sky. Then the golden rim of the sun itself rested on a mountain top; the door of the hall crashed open, the wizard bounced in.

The wizard looked around him – no princess! He gave a scream of laughter, and strode towards the prince . . .

But Sharpsight saw him and told Long. Long gave one mighty stride. Sharpsight fixed his fiery eyes on one of the hall windows, the glass shivered into pieces, and Long flung the ring into the hall.

The ring dropped to the floor, and vanished. There stood the princess. When the wizard saw her, he gave a roar that shook the castle, and *bang!* the last iron hoop that girdled his waist burst and fell off him. The wizard turned into a black raven, spread his wings, gave a loud croak, and flew out through the shattered window.

Then the pale cheeks of the princess turned rosy, and her sorrowful eyes shone with joy. She ran to the prince and kissed his hand; but the prince took her in his arms and kissed her rosy lips. In the castle everything came alive: knights and princes, squires and grooms gathered in the hall and crowded round the prince and princess, cheering and blessing them. In the stables the stone horses became flesh and blood, and stamped and whinnied. Out in the desolate country the trees put forth leaves, grass covered the barren earth, blossoms sprang up on every side, the river flowed with a contented murmur between flowery banks, thrushes and blackbirds sang among the trees, and high overhead larks poured down a silver rain of song.

'*Hurrah! Hurrah! Hurrah!*' The grooms ran to the stables, horses were saddled and bridled, and in a mighty company the prince and the princess, the knights and the squires and the grooms, and Long, Broad and Sharpsight set off for the prince's home.

The king had never thought to see his son again. He had become bowed down with grief. But now he rose up and clothed himself in joy, as the trees about the iron castle had clothed themselves in green leaves. Bonfires blazed, fireworks cracked, the people feasted, the fountains of the city ran with wine. The princess laughed and clapped her hands. There was a grand wedding, you may be sure!

After the wedding, Long, Broad and Sharpsight came to bid the prince good-bye. The prince urged them to stay with him; but no, they did not want to lead an idle life; they would go out into the world and look for more work. So off they went; and the first good work that Sharpsight did was to fix his fiery eyes upon the iron castle and raze it to the ground.

Somewhere or other, so we are told, Long, Broad and Sharpsight are still wandering about the world, and if you are lucky you may chance one day to meet them. But as for the wizard, where he has gone to no one knows. He has never been seen again.

4 · Gold

Once upon a time there was a young man who owned a small tumbledown farm. He lived alone, far from any village, and about a mile from a sheet of water called the Green Lake.

Well, one autumn evening, an old fellow wearing a ragged black cloak, and carrying an empty sack, knocked at this farmer's door.

'Friend,' said he, 'may I crave a night's lodging?'

'Surely!' said the farmer. 'Step in.'

The old fellow in the ragged black cloak stepped in. The farmer set supper before him, and afterwards took him to a small room where there was a bed; and there he slept.

In the morning, the old fellow rose early.

'Friend,' said he, 'I must go on my way. As you see, I am poor and ragged. I have nothing to offer you but my blessing; and that you shall have.' Then he took up his empty sack and walked off towards the Green Lake.

The farmer never gave the old fellow another thought. But, during the year that followed, everything prospered with him. His cattle were sleeker and glossier than they had ever been before; his cows gave twice as much milk, and that milk was thick with cream; and every ewe in his little flock bore twins. The farmer put money by, and was able to repair his tumbledown farm.

Next autumn, exactly a year to the day, the old fellow in the ragged black cloak knocked at the farmer's door again, and again asked for a night's lodging. The farmer was able this time to give him a better supper and a better bed. And in the morning the old

fellow blessed him again, picked up his empty sack, and walked off towards the Green Lake.

Again for a year the farmer prospered exceedingly. His flocks and herds increased; he bought more land, and was able to hire labourers to help him, and a housekeeper to look after him. 'I am indeed greatly blessed!' he thought.

And then he remembered the old fellow in the ragged black cloak, and how he had said, 'I leave you my blessing.' 'Who can he be?' he wondered. 'And will he come again?'

The old fellow in the ragged black cloak did come again. He

came on an autumn evening as he had done before. And as before he asked for a night's lodging. The farmer bade him welcome, and told his housekeeper to provide the very best supper she could. And when supper was over, he leaned across the table and said, 'Friend, who and what are you?'

'A blessing to those whom I bless, and a curse to those whom I curse,' answered he of the ragged black cloak.

The farmer felt frightened. 'Surely this man must be a wizard,' he thought. And he asked no more questions.

But in the morning, when the old fellow had bidden him good-bye and blessed him, and taken up his sack and gone on his way towards the Green Lake, the farmer followed – for he was overcome with curiosity. Near the lake was a fountain, and under the fountain was a wooden trough into which the spring from the fountain was running. And not far from the wooden trough was a little thicket of alder trees.

And the farmer hid himself in the thicket and watched.

The old fellow in the ragged black cloak went to the trough, lifted a stone slab which covered it, plunged his hands into the water, and began drawing out of it something that looked like bright sand. He filled his sack with the sand; and when the sack was full, he put the stone slab back over the trough, hoisted the sack on to his shoulder, and walked away.

The farmer, peeping through the alders, watched him walking away and away: round by the lake, and through the valley, and up over a grassy hill. He watched till the old fellow became a tiny speck in the distance; he watched till he could see him no more; and then he came out of the alder thicket.

'There must be some value in that sand,' he said to himself, 'or the old fellow wouldn't come so far to fetch it again and again.'

And he went over to the trough, lifted the stone slab and plunged his hands into the water to pick up what lay beneath it.

Heavens above! It was not sand – it was gold dust!

The farmer ran home, took a shovel and the largest sack he could find, and hastened back to the trough. He shovelled up gold dust till the sack was bursting full, and was so heavy that he could barely lift it. Then he dragged the sack into the alder thicket, and hid it.

All that day he could do no work at all for thinking of his sack of gold. When night came, and his housekeeper had gone to bed, he tiptoed out to the stable, bridled his stoutest horse, and rode down to the Green Lake. In the alder thicket it was pitch dark, but the farmer groped about, found his sack, and puffing and panting under its weight, hoisted it on to his horse's back. Then he led the horse to the farm, hid the sack under a pile of straw in the stable, and went to bed – to lie awake all night thinking of his treasure.

In the morning he told his housekeeper that he had a sackful of good grain to spare, and that he was going to the capital of the country to sell it. And so, with his sack of gold strapped on to the back of one horse, and himself riding another, he set off.

It took him three days to reach the capital, and by the time he reached it he was worn out; for he had not been able to sleep at the inns where he put up, for worrying lest someone should discover what was in his sack, and steal it. But no one did steal it.

In the city he sought out the richest merchant, had the sack carried into the office behind the merchant's shop, and, when the door was closed and he and the merchant were alone together, he opened the sack and offered the gold for sale.

'My good man!' said the merchant, 'I have not enough money in the world to buy all this gold! Nor, I am sure, have any of my fellow merchants. You must go down the street to that large house at the corner. It is shut up and looks as if nobody lives there. But knock, and the richest man in the country will let you in. Perhaps he will buy your gold – but I cannot be certain. He is a man of strange whims.'

So the farmer fastened up his sack again, and the merchant sent two servants with him to carry the sack to the large house at the corner of the street. The house certainly did look as if no one lived there: every window was closed, every shutter drawn. But when the farmer reached it, he heard a voice calling from somewhere inside, 'Farmer, bring here your gold! Open the door and come in.'

The farmer opened the door and went in. The servants put down the sack of gold inside the door and went away. The farmer gazed round him in amazement. What splendour, what riches! He was in a great hall hung with cloth of gold and glittering with jewels, and the stairway that wound up at the back of the hall seemed to be cut out of one huge rainbow-coloured crystal.

'Farmer, come up!' called the voice.

The farmer tiptoed up the stairs, and saw before him a door of many coloured jasper.

'Farmer, come in!' called the voice.

The farmer went in through the door. Now he was in a round room that glimmered like a pearl. It had a silver dome, and from the dome hung a crystal lamp burning with a milky flame which sent out sweet odours. But the farmer had no eyes for all this splendour – for there, on a golden throne under the lamp, sat he of the black ragged cloak. But he was not now wearing the black ragged cloak; he was dressed in a rich robe patterned with suns, moons and stars, and on his head was a pointed hat blazing with jewels. His hands were on his knees, and between his hands was a large crystal globe.

'Farmer,' said the wizard, for such indeed he was, 'you have not dealt honestly with me. Did I not bless you with prosperity enough, but you must needs clear out my trough? The gold that you have brought me is my own; and as my own I keep it. But since you have three times fed and sheltered me, I will pay you for your three days' journey. Yes, I have watched you every step of your way, and your way has been an anxious one. Here are three pieces of gold for you: one piece for each day's journey. Come,

44

stand by me and look into my globe. I will show you your journey home.'

The trembling farmer stepped up to the wizard's side, and looked down into the globe. The globe seemed to be full of clouds, that gathered and parted and gathered again.

'Look steadily,' said the wizard. 'The clouds will pass.'

The farmer looked steadily, and the clouds vanished. There, small, but very bright and clear, he saw a sandy-coloured road winding away out of the city, now between cornfields, now up wooded hills, now down into green valleys. And he saw, travelling along that road, the figure of a man who rode one horse and led another. The man was himself. He saw the man that was himself enter a village, put up at an inn, sup and go to bed, to sleep soundly, untroubled by fear of thieves. He saw the whole of his three days' journey home.

And then he saw his farm, with labourers reaping in the fields, and his housekeeper busy in the kitchen. He saw, too, the Green Lake, lying in the valley below his farm; but he saw neither fountain nor trough. Where they had been, a bright stream bubbled up out of the ground and flowed into the lake. Then everything faded; and in the globe he saw only the swiftly moving clouds, gathering and parting, and gathering again.

'Now go home, farmer,' said the wizard. 'You will never see my fountain or my trough again. I am saving you from further temptation. But work hard, and you shall continue to prosper. I will remain a blessing to you, not a curse.'

Without a word the farmer went out of the wizard's house, paid his score at the inn, took his two horses, and rode thoughtfully home. With the three pieces of gold that the wizard had given him, he paid for his three nights' lodging on the way. When he reached his farm, his pockets were empty, but his heart was light.

The wizard never came to visit him again; nor, when he went down to the Green Lake, was there any sign of the fountain or the trough. There was only the bright little stream bubbling up out of the ground and flowing into the lake. He never told a soul about his adventure; but he worked hard, and he continued to prosper, as the wizard had promised. He married a buxom country lass, and by and by had a houseful of merry children.

And all went well with him to his life's end.

5 · Farmer Weathersky

A man and his wife had a son called Jack. One day Jack's mother said to Jack's father, 'Old man, it's time our Jack went out and learned a trade. So be off, both of you, and see about it. But, mind you, Jack must be apprenticed to someone who will teach him to be a master above all masters.'

Then Jack's mother put some food and a roll of tobacco into a bag, and off went Jack and his father.

They went a long way; but, dear me, could they find any one who would teach Jack to be a master above all masters? No, they could not. Many a man said he could teach Jack to be as good at his trade as he was himself; but more than that no one would promise to do. So Jack and his father went home again.

Jack's mother wasn't pleased to see them back. 'Old man,' said she, 'I don't care what trade Jack learns; but this I say, and this I stick to – he must be taught to be a master above all masters.'

Then she packed up some more food and another roll of tobacco, and sent them off again.

They walked and they walked; it was very cold, and by and by they came to a plain that was covered with ice. And there was a man whisking along in a sledge, drawn by a black horse.

'Whither away?' said the man in the sledge.

'To apprentice my son to someone,' said Jack's father. 'But my old woman has such grand notions that nothing will content her but he must learn to be a master above all masters. And who can teach him that?'

'Well, *I* can,' said the man in the sledge, 'and I'm in need of an apprentice. So up with you, Jack!'

Jack got up into the sledge, and *whisk!* off they went, man, Jack, sledge and horse, right up into the air.

'Stop! Stop!' cried Jack's father. 'You haven't told me your name, nor where your home is!'

And the man in the sledge called down, 'Oh, I'm at home north, east, south and west, and my name is Farmer Weathersky. Come here again in a year and a day, and you shall hear whether Jack suits me or no.'

Jack's father went home; he was sorely troubled.

'Well, old man,' said Jack's mother. 'I see you've found a master for Jack this time. Who is he, and where does he live?'

'Heaven knows,' said Jack's father, 'for I'm sure I don't!'

And he told her what had happened.

'Up into the sky, indeed, a likely story!' said Jack's mother. 'You go off again, and don't you come back till you've found out where our Jack is.'

And she gave him another bag of food and another roll of tobacco, and packed him off once more.

He walked and he walked, and he came to a great wood. He was all day walking through that wood – there seemed no end to it. But at nightfall he came to a little house under a rock. And outside the house was an old hag, drawing up water from a well with her long, long nose.

'Good evening, mother!' said he.

'Good evening to you!' said the old hag. 'It's hundreds of years since anyone called me mother.'

'Can I stay here for the night?' said he.

'No, you can't,' said she.

Then Jack's father pulled out his roll of tobacco, filled his pipe and lit it.

'Like a whiff?' said he.

48

'That I would,' said she.

And when she had taken a whiff or two at the pipe, and a pinch or two of some snuff which he also gave her, the old hag was so happy that she began to dance.

'You are a man after my own heart!' said she. 'You can stay the night.'

And she gave him some supper and a bed.

In the morning he said, 'Have you ever heard tell of Farmer Weathersky?'

'Not I,' said she. 'But maybe my beasts will know of him.'

She took a horn and blew three loud blasts, and all the beasts in the world came galloping, till the wood was full of them.

But none of them knew anything about Farmer Weathersky.

'Well!' said the old hag. 'There are three sisters of us. Maybe one of the other two will know where he lives. I'll lend you my horse and sledge to go to my second sister. She lives three hundred miles away; but you'll be there before night.'

That was a horse, and that was a sledge! Jack's father got into the sledge and the horse galloped off. If the horse had flown he couldn't have gone faster, and by evening they reached the second old hag's house, which stood on the sea shore. This old hag also had a long, long nose, and what was she doing but raking up sea-weed with it.

'Good evening, mother,' said Jack's father.

'Good evening to you,' said the second old hag. 'It's hundreds of years since anyone called me mother.'

'Can I stay here for the night?' said he.

'No, you can't,' said she.

But he lit his pipe and gave her a whiff, and also some snuff. Then she was so happy that she began to jump for joy.

Said she, 'You are a man after my own heart! You can stay the night.'

And she took him in and gave him supper and a bed.

In the morning he asked if she had ever heard tell of Farmer Weathersky. No, she hadn't; but maybe one of her fishes might have. She gave three loud blasts on a horn to call her fishes home, and they came till the sea was solid with them.

But none of them knew anything about Farmer Weathersky.

So the old hag lent Jack's father her boat and her swiftest dolphin, and sent him off to the third sister's house. It was six hundred miles away, but the dolphin sped over the waves so fast that they reached the house before nightfall.

The house door was open, and Jack's father went in. There he found the third old hag standing before the hearth. And what was she doing but stirring the fire with her nose, so long and tough it was.

'Good evening, mother!'

'Good evening to you! It's hundreds of years since anyone called me mother.'

'Can I stay the night here?'

'No, you can't.'

But Jack's father lit his pipe and gave her a whiff, and also a pinch or two of snuff. Then she was so happy that she danced and sang.

'You are a man after my own heart!' said she. 'You can stay the night and welcome.'

So she gave him supper and a bed.

In the morning he asked after Farmer Weathersky. No, she had never heard of him; but maybe her birds might know. She blew three loud blasts on a horn, and all the birds of the air came flying – the sky was dark with them. No, none of them knew anything of Farmer Weathersky.

'I don't see my big eagle,' said the old hag.

She blew another blast on her horn, and waited. She blew another blast, and yet another. At last, there was her big eagle dropping through the air. He was so weary that he could scarcely flap his wings; but he knew all about Farmer Weathersky and where he lived; he had just come from his house.

The old hag said, 'You must take this man there.'

The eagle said, 'I can't, until I've had something to eat and a night's rest.'

Well, the eagle had some food and a night's rest, and next morning the old hag pulled a feather out of the eagle's tail, and put Jack's father in the place where the feather had been.

'Now be off!' she said.

The eagle flew and flew and flew. He flew fast, but they didn't reach Farmer Weathersky's house until midnight. And Farmer Weathersky was snoring so loudly that the house rocked.

'Go into the kitchen,' said the eagle. 'Open the table drawer and take out three crumbs of bread. You'll find Farmer Weathersky in bed. You must pull three feathers out of his head – he won't wake up.'

Jack's father went into the kitchen, opened the table drawer, and took out three breadcrumbs. Then he tiptoed over to Farmer Weathersky's bed. Farmer Weathersky was lying on his back with his mouth open; he was rocking the house with his snores. He had feathers growing out of his head instead of hair. Jack's father pulled out a feather.

'Oof!' growled Farmer Weathersky. But he didn't wake up.

Jack's father pulled out a second feather.

'OOF!' growled Farmer Weathersky. But still he didn't wake.

Jack's father pulled out the third feather.

'OOF!' Farmer Weathersky let out such a roar that part of the roof fell off. But he didn't wake for all that. And Jack's father went out with the feathers.

Then the eagle told him what to do next. And this is what he did. He went into the house yard, and there at the stable door he found a big black stone. He lifted up the stone, and under it he found three chips of wood. He picked up the chips and knocked at the stable door. The door opened of itself. He went into the stable and threw down the three breadcrumbs. A hare came and ate up the crumbs, and he caught the hare and kept it. Then he went back to the eagle.

'Good!' said the eagle. 'Now pull some more feathers out of my tail, and put yourself, and the hare, and the chips of wood, and the black stone, and the feathers from Farmer Weathersky's head in the place of my feathers.'

Jack's father did that. The eagle spread his wings and flew back on the way home. He flew a long way; then he got tired and alighted down on a rock to rest. After he had rested for a bit, he said, 'Do you see anything?'

'Yes,' said Jack's father. 'I see a flock of crows coming this way.'

'We'd best be off then,' said the eagle. And he flew on. He flew a long way. 'Do you see anything now?' he said.

'Yes, the crows are close behind us.'

'Drop the three feathers you pulled out of Farmer Weathersky's head,' said the eagle.

Jack's father dropped the three feathers. They turned into a flock of ravens and drove the crows home again.

The eagle flew on. He flew a long way; then he got tired again and alighted down on a rock. 'Do you see anything?' he said.

'I see something, but it's very far away.'

'We'd best be off then,' said the eagle. And he flew on.

He flew and he flew. 'Do you see anything now?' he asked.

'Yes,' said Jack's father. 'I see Farmer Weathersky rushing through the air close behind us.'

'Drop the chips of wood,' said the eagle.

Jack's father dropped the chips of wood. They took fire and blazed from earth to heaven.

Farmer Weathersky couldn't get through that fire. He had to go home for a pail of water to put it out.

The eagle flew on. He flew and he flew. He got tired and alighted down on a fir tree to rest. 'Do you see anything?' he asked.

'Well! I'm not sure. I think there is something, but it's very far away.'

'We'd best be off then,' said the eagle. And on he flew.

He flew and he flew. Then he said, 'Do you see anything now?'

'Yes, I see Farmer Weathersky rushing close behind us.'

'Drop the big black stone you lifted up at the stable door.'

Jack's father dropped the stone. It turned into a black fog that stretched from earth to heaven. Farmer Weathersky was pushing his way through the fog, but he couldn't see where he was going. He stumbled and fell to earth and broke his leg. So he had to go home and splint it. And by the time he had done that, the eagle had reached Jack's home.

'Put the hare on the ground,' said the eagle.

Jack's father put the hare on the ground. It turned into Jack.

Then the eagle flew away, and Jack and his father went in-doors.

Well, well, Jack's mother was overjoyed to see them. 'But what have you learned?' she said to Jack. 'Are you a master above all masters?'

'I should be,' said Jack, 'for Farmer Weathersky is a mighty wizard, and what I didn't learn from him isn't worth learning.'

His mother wasn't satisfied. She wanted a proof that Jack was a master above all masters.

Said Jack, 'I'll give you a proof in the morning.'

So next morning Jack got up early and turned himself into a bay horse. 'Now,' said he to his father, 'you can lead me to market and sell me. You may ask a hundred dollars for me. But mind you don't sell my halter. You must take that off and keep it. If you don't keep it, Farmer Weathersky will keep *me*; for it is he who will come to buy me.'

Jack's father led the bay horse to market. And up came Farmer

Weathersky disguised as a merchant. 'I'll give you a hundred dollars for that horse.'

'Done!'

Farmer Weathersky handed over the money. Jack's father pocketed it, and took the halter off the horse.

Said Father Weathersky, 'Give me the halter.'

Said Jack's father, 'That wasn't in the bargain. Besides, I need it. I have other horses to bring to market tomorrow.' And off he went on his way home with the halter.

When he got home he found that Jack had arrived before him. There he was, sitting in the ingle.

Next day Jack turned himself into a brown horse, and said, 'Now father, lead me to market. You can ask two hundred dollars for me, but mind you keep my halter!'

So Jack's father led the brown horse to market. And up came Farmer Weathersky, disguised as a merchant.

'How much for the brown horse?'

'Two hundred dollars.'

'Done!' Farmer Weathersky handed over the money. Jack's father pocketed it.

'But I want the halter,' said Farmer Weathersky.

'That wasn't in the bargain. Besides, I need it.'

So off went Jack's father with the halter, and off went Farmer Weathersky with the brown horse. And he hadn't gone far when the brown horse gave Farmer Weathersky a kick, galloped off, and turned into Jack. When Jack's father got home, there was Jack sitting in the ingle.

Next morning Jack turned himself into a black horse, and his father led him to market. 'Three hundred dollars is the price you'll get for me today,' said the horse, 'but don't forget about my halter.'

'No, I won't forget,' said Jack's father.

In the market, there was Farmer Weathersky with a disguise on him. He was willing to pay three hundred dollars for the black horse, but said he must have the halter.

Jack's father said, 'No.' Farmer Weathersky said, 'Yes.' He offered a hundred dollars for the halter. Jack's father said, 'No.' Farmer Weathersky offered two hundred, three hundred, four hundred dollars. Jack's father still said, 'No.' But when Farmer Weathersky came to five hundred dollars, the father's greed got the better of him, and he said, 'Very well, take it!' Thought he, 'If Jack's so clever, surely he can slip a halter off his head!' So he went home with eight hundred dollars.

And Farmer Weathersky took the halter rope in his hand, and led the black horse away.

Farmer Weathersky walked on, leading the black horse, till he came to an inn. Then he felt hungry and thought he would go inside and have a bite. He put a barrel of red-hot nails under the horse's nose, and a bucket full of oats behind his tail, tied the halter rope to a hook by the door, and went into the inn.

The black horse whinnied and stamped and reared; he made such a noise that a little serving maid came to the door to see what it was all about.

'Oh, you poor beastie!' said the little serving maid. 'What a cruel master you must have to treat you so!'

And she untied the halter rope so that the black horse could turn round and eat the oats.

The black horse put down his head, and tore and tore at the halter with his hoof till he broke it. And no sooner had he shaken himself free of that halter than Farmer Weathersky came rushing out.

'I'M AFTER YOU!' roared Farmer Weathersky.

But the black horse jumped into a duck pond and turned himself into a little fish. Farmer Weathersky jumped into the duck pond and turned himself into a huge pike. The little fish leaped out of the duck pond, turned itself into a dove, and flew away. The pike leaped out of the pond, turned itself into a hawk, and gave chase.

What a chase! The dove was swift, but the hawk was swifter. The dove had a start, but the hawk was gaining on it. The dove came flying to a palace, and there was a princess looking out of a window.

'Ah, poor dove!' she cried.

She opened the window, the dove flew in, and turned into Jack.

The hawk flew to the ground, turned into Farmer Weathersky, and went into the palace.

'Turn yourself into a gold ring, Jack, and put yourself on my finger,' said the princess.

'No, no,' said Jack, 'that won't do. Farmer Weathersky will make the king sick; and there'll be no one who can make him well again, till Farmer Weathersky turns himself into a doctor and cures him. And for his fee he'll ask for the ring off your finger.'

'But I'll say I had it from my mother and can't part with it!' said the princess.

So then Jack turned himself into a gold ring, and put himself on the princess's finger. And it fell out just as Jack had said. Farmer Weathersky laid a spell on the king and made him sick, and not a doctor could cure him. Then Farmer Weathersky turned himself into a doctor and went to the king. 'I can cure you,' he said. 'But first pay me my fee. My fee is the gold ring that the princess wears on her finger.'

The king was lying in bed. He sent a messenger to the princess to ask for the ring.

The princess said, 'I have other rings of greater value than this one. The doctor can take his choice among them. But this ring I will not part with, for it was left me by my mother.'

Farmer Weathersky said, 'I will have the gold ring from the princess's finger, and no other.'

The king sent again to the princess. No, she wouldn't part with that ring. The king sent many times. It was always 'No, no!' from the princess. Then the king flew into a rage, and said he would have that ring, he didn't care *who* had given it to the princess.

So the princess came to the king and said, 'It's no use your being cross, Papa. I can't get the ring off my finger. If you want the ring, you'll have to take my finger also.'

'If you'll let *me* try, I'll soon get it off,' said Farmer Weathersky.

'Don't you dare touch me!' said the princess. 'If anyone must try, I'll try myself.'

Then she ran to the grate, and put ashes on her finger. And the ring slipped off and fell among the ashes. Then Farmer Weathersky turned himself into a cock, and went to scrape among the ashes. He was there scratching and scraping till he was covered with ashes up to the eyes. But just when his beak touched the ring, the ring turned itself into a fox; the fox gave one snap – off went the cock's head. Then the fox spat the ashes out of his mouth, and turned into Jack.

Now that Farmer Weathersky was dead, the king got well at once. He jumped out of bed. He was so delighted that when the princess said she wanted to marry Jack, he said, 'Anything you like, my dear.'

So they were married, and lived happily. Jack built his parents a fine house to live in; and whatever else they wanted they had only to ask him for, and he produced it immediately. So Jack's mother was now satisfied that she had a son who was a master above all masters.

6 · Aladdin

(1) THE IDLE BOY

Once upon a time, and far away in an eastern country, there lived a very idle boy, called Aladdin. His father was a poor tailor, and he tried to teach Aladdin his trade. But Aladdin wouldn't learn. No sooner was his father's back turned than the naughty boy was off and out into the streets. He did nothing but romp about and get into mischief. And this so grieved his father that he fell ill and died.

Then Aladdin's mother wept and said, 'Surely now you will mend your ways, or we shall starve!'

But Aladdin wouldn't mend his ways, and his poor mother had scarcely enough to buy bread.

Well, one day when Aladdin was playing in the streets as usual a stranger passed by. The stranger looked at Aladdin and muttered, 'That is the lad for me!' He went up to a butcher who was standing at the door of his shop, and said, 'Tell me, sir, who is that boy in the ragged turban?'

'That,' said the butcher, 'is the son of Mustapha the tailor. As you see, he is a good-for-nothing. His father died of grief because of his idle ways.'

'Tut, tut! Is it possible?' said the stranger.

Now you must know that this stranger was a mighty wizard, who had flown all the way from Africa, seeking for a boy to serve his ends. He kept his eye on Aladdin, and the moment he found him alone, he went up to him and said, 'Surely you must be the son of Mustapha the tailor?'

'So I am,' said Aladdin. 'What of it?'

Wasn't Aladdin astonished when the wizard flung his arms round him and kissed him many times!

'Oh my dear, dear boy,' he said, 'heaven be praised that I have found you! I am your uncle, your father's brother – you are as like him as one pearl is like to another! Come, let us hasten – take me to your father!'

'Well, I can't do that,' said Aladdin, 'because he is dead.'

Then the wizard wept. 'Dead – oh no! I have come all the way from Africa to find him, and you say he is dead! Oh, my boy, what a terrible blow! But here – take these few small coins. Go quickly to your mother. Give her my love, and tell her I will come to visit her tomorrow.'

Aladdin ran home. 'Mother, I have just seen my uncle.'

'Oh my boy, what will you say next? You have no uncle!'

'But he told me he was my father's brother. He cried and kissed me. He gave me some money, and sent you his love. He said he would visit us tomorrow.'

'Indeed, indeed,' said Aladdin's mother. 'This is very strange!'

Next day the wizard found Aladdin in the streets again. He gave him two gold pieces. 'Take these to your mother,' he said. 'Tell her I will visit her this evening, and bid her buy something for supper. But show me first where you live.'

Aladdin pointed out his mother's poor little house, and the wizard said, 'Ah! Ah! It was high time I came home to help you!'

Aladdin took the two gold pieces to his mother. She went out and bought food, and spent all day preparing the supper.

In the evening the wizard came, bringing quantities of fruit and wine. He embraced Aladdin's mother and said, 'My dear sister, you mustn't be surprised that you have never seen me. For forty years I have travelled abroad. But come, show me the place where my brother used to sit.'

'There on the sofa,' said she. 'Pray sit there yourself.'

But the wizard fell on his knees and kissed the sofa.

'Alas, my poor brother!' he wept. 'No, no, heaven forbid that I should take your place! But allow me, sister, to take this seat opposite the sofa, so that if I may not behold my brother, I may at least behold the place where he used to sit.'

By this time the wizard had quite won the heart of Aladdin's mother. And when they had eaten their supper he said to Aladdin, 'What is your trade, nephew? Are you a tailor like your father?'

Aladdin hung his head, and his mother answered, 'Oh brother, Aladdin does no work at all! His father tried to teach him his trade but he wouldn't learn. He spends all his time in the streets with bad companions. He is an idle wretch, and I have almost made up my mind to turn him out of doors.'

With that, the poor woman burst into tears.

The wizard turned to Aladdin and said, 'Nephew, this is not right. You must think of helping yourself and your mother. But perhaps your father's trade does not appeal to you? Come now, how would you like to keep a shop? I will take one for you and stock it with all sorts of fine stuffs. What do you say?'

Yes, Aladdin would like to keep a shop. He thanked the wizard. As to his mother, it seemed to the poor woman that all her troubles were at an end.

The next day the wizard took Aladdin to a clothier's. 'As you are so soon to become a merchant,' he said, 'you must be fittingly dressed. Come, choose for yourself.'

The delighted Aladdin chose the finest clothes he could see, and when he was dressed in them he felt grand as a prince. And indeed, he was a handsome lad, and looked very well in his finery. He strutted and flaunted like any peacock – and his poor mother prayed heaven to rain down blessings on her supposed brother-in-law's noble head.

(II) THE UNDERGROUND PALACE

Next morning the wizard came yet again for Aladdin.

'Today, nephew, we will go into the country and enjoy ourselves. And tomorrow we will see about taking a shop for you.'

Off they set, and after walking far beyond the city walls, they came to a beautiful garden. Here they sat to rest by a fountain. The wizard pulled from his girdle a handkerchief filled with cakes and fruit. And whilst they were eating he gave Aladdin a little lecture, telling him he would soon be a man, and that he must promise in future to avoid bad company.

'I will indeed, uncle,' said Aladdin. 'I will do my best to please you – you are so good to me!'

So, when they were rested, on they went, and walked until they came to a narrow valley between two mountains.

'Now I will show you something wonderful,' said the wizard. 'But first gather a bundle of dry sticks that we may light a fire.'

Aladdin collected the sticks. The wizard lit a fire. He took a white powder from his purse, muttered some words that Aladdin did not understand, and threw the powder on the fire.

Immediately the ground opened, and there at the wizard's feet was a big flat stone with a brass ring fastened to it. Aladdin was frightened; he would have run away, but the wizard caught him by the arm and shook him roughly.

'You fool of a boy!' he cried. 'Am I not your uncle? Can you not trust me? Obey me, and your fortune is made; but I will have nothing to do with cowards! Under this stone lies a treasure that will make you richer than the greatest monarch of the world. Now, if you are brave enough, take hold of the ring, lift the stone, and fetch your fortune!'

At the word 'fortune' Aladdin forgot his fears. He took hold of the ring, gave a pull – and the stone came up quite easily.

Under the stone there were steps going down, and there was a closed door at the foot of the steps.

'Go down, nephew,' said the wizard. 'Open that door. It will lead you into a palace, divided into three great halls. At the end of the third hall you will come into a garden planted with fruit trees. Walk across the garden to a terrace where you will see a niche, and on the niche a lighted lamp. Take down the lamp, empty out the oil, and bring the lamp to me.'

'And the fortune, uncle?' said Aladdin.

'Ah, the fortune,' chuckled the wizard. 'That will be given to you when you have brought up the lamp.'

He then placed a ring on Aladdin's finger. 'This ring will protect you from all harm,' he said; 'but only as long as you obey me. Go forward, be bold, and prosper!'

Aladdin went down the steps, opened the door at the bottom, and came into the palace with three halls. He passed through the halls into the garden planted with fruit trees, walked through the garden to the terrace, lifted down the lamp from its niche, emptied out the oil, and thrust the lamp into the front of his robe, tying his sash tightly beneath it.

On his way back through the garden, he paused to admire the trees, which were glittering with fruit of every colour. He reached up to pick some of the fruits: but to his disappointment he found they were stones. Indeed, though he did not know it, they were jewels of immense value. Aladdin would have preferred figs or dates. Still, he thought he would take some of the various coloured stones to show to his mother. So he thrust into the front of his robe as many jewels as it would hold. Then he went back through the three halls and climbed up the steps.

The top step was a yard or so below the hole in the earth. Aladdin reached up his hands and grasped the edge of the hole. 'Uncle!' he called. 'Help me out!'

'Have you got the lamp?' shouted the wizard.

'Yes, uncle.'

'Then hand it up!'

Now the lamp was wedged down tightly under all the stones Aladdin had packed into his robe, so he shouted, 'No, uncle, I can't. My hands are not free. I'll give it to you when I get out.'

'You must hand up the lamp first!' cried the wizard.

'No, uncle, I've told you, I can't.'

The wizard stamped with rage. 'Hand it up! Hand it up!'

'No, uncle. I feel giddy here in the dark. I shall fall!'

'Hand up that lamp!'

'No, uncle!'

The wizard began to stamp and shriek. Aladdin felt frightened. He thought his uncle must be crazy. He tried to scramble out of the hole, but the wizard pushed him back.

'At least I will have that ring I gave you!' screamed the wizard, and he tried to snatch it off Aladdin's finger. But Aladdin's fingers were clinging tightly to the edges of the hole. The wizard couldn't get the ring off. At last, mad with rage, he threw some more powder on the fire, and said two magic words: the stone moved back and covered the hole, and there was Aladdin, buried in the dark.

'Uncle! Uncle!'

But the wizard spread out his robe on either side of him like wings, flew up into the air, and never stopped flying until he reached Africa.

Then indeed Aladdin, as he wept and hammered at the stone with his fists, knew at last that this pretended kind uncle was no other than a wicked wizard. But what good was that knowledge to him now? And why had the wizard wanted the lamp?

What Aladdin could not know was that the wizard had read in
his magic book of a wonderful lamp that would make him the
most powerful man in the world. By his spells he had found out
where the lamp was, and learned, too, that he could only receive
it from the hands of another person. And so he had flown from
Africa, and picked out poor foolish Aladdin to serve his ends,
meaning to get the lamp from him, push him back into the hole
and leave him there to die.

Aladdin beat at the stone till his fists were sore; then he groped
his way down the steps and felt for the door. 'Perhaps if I can get
into the garden I shall find another way out,' he thought.

But the door had slammed shut, and there was no opening it.

'Oh, what shall I do? What shall I do?' he wailed.

He sat with his head in his hands and rocked himself to and fro.
He clapped his hands together, felt the ring the wizard had given

him, and in disgust thought to pull it off his finger. But no sooner had he rubbed that ring than there came a flash of light, and an enormous genie rose out of the earth.

'What wouldest thou?' said the genie. 'I am the Slave of the Ring, and will obey thee in all things.'

'Oh, take me out of here, whoever you are!' cried Aladdin.

He had scarcely said the words before he found himself in the valley between the two mountains, standing on the very spot where the wizard had kindled the fire. The fire had gone, the hole in the earth had gone. There was nothing but the smooth, grassy ground. Aladdin set off running, and ran and ran till he reached home. And there, at his mother's door, he fell down in a faint.

(III) THE SLAVE OF THE LAMP

When Aladdin's mother had brought him to his senses with burnt feathers and plenty of cold water, he told her all that had happened. Then he asked for some food.

'Alas, my poor boy,' said his mother, 'I have not even a bit of bread to give you. But I have spun a little cotton and will go out and sell it.'

'No,' said Aladdin, 'keep your cotton for another time. Here is this old lamp. I will go out and sell that.'

His mother looked at the lamp, and seeing it was very dirty, said she would clean it. 'It will fetch more if I can get a polish on it,' she said.

She took some sand and water to clean the lamp; but no sooner had she given it one rub, than there was a flash of light, and an enormous genie rose out of the ground.

'What wouldest thou?' said the genie. 'I am the Slave of the Lamp, and will obey thee in all things.'

'No, no! Go away!' cried the terrified woman, and flung up her arm before her eyes.

But Aladdin snatched the lamp from her. 'I am hungry,' he said. 'Bring me something to eat.'

The genie vanished and at once appeared again, carrying a silver tray on which were twelve silver dishes filled with delicious food, also six large cakes, two flagons of wine, and two silver cups. He placed the tray down on the carpet and disappeared.

'Come, mother, eat!' cried Aladdin.

That was a meal! They ate till they could eat no more, and then they had enough over to last them all next day. And when the food was gone, Aladdin sold the silver dishes, and bought more food. And when that was gone, he rubbed the lamp again, and bade the genie bring them food and clothes and everything that they needed.

'Mother,' he said, 'we shall never want again. We have two slaves to serve us with all that we can desire: the Slave of the Lamp, and the Slave of the Ring.'

But his mother shook her head. She begged him to throw away both the ring and the lamp, and take up an honest trade. 'Mark my words,' she said. 'No good will come of trafficking with devils. And what else can these two be?'

Aladdin laughed at her fears. He would not part with either the ring or the lamp. He had only to rub the one or the other to get anything he wanted; and so he and his mother lived in comfort for several years.

(IV) THE PRINCESS

And Aladdin grew up. He no longer wanted to romp about the streets. He would now like to improve himself, and he visited the shops of the merchants, listened to their talk, examined their wares, and to his astonishment learned that the fruits which he had plucked from the trees in the underground garden, and which he had thought to be coloured pebbles, were in reality precious gems of the utmost value. He saw that none of the merchants had jewels to equal them.

One day, as he was walking in the city, a herald passed through the streets ordering all the people to close their shutters and keep within doors whilst the sultan's daughter went to and from the bath-house. Aladdin thought he would like to see the princess's face, for he had heard that she was very beautiful. But it wasn't easy to see her face, because she always went veiled.

So what did Aladdin do but hide himself behind the door of the bath-house and peep through a chink. The princess lifted her veil as she went in, and she looked so beautiful that Aladdin fell in love with her there and then.

When he went home he was so pale and thoughtful that his mother said, 'What is the matter? Are you ill?'

'No, I am not ill,' said Aladdin. 'But I have seen the princess. I love her so deeply that I cannot live without her. I will ask her in marriage from the sultan.'

His mother burst out laughing. 'What are you saying, Aladdin? You must be mad!'

But Aladdin said, 'Why shouldn't I marry the princess? I have the Slave of the Lamp and the Slave of the Ring to help me. And, what's more, those stones that I plucked from the trees in the garden are jewels fit for the greatest monarch. I will offer them to the sultan, and I'm sure he will favour me. You have a fine porcelain dish. Fetch it, and let us see how the jewels look in it.'

Aladdin's mother brought the dish; Aladdin fetched the jewels and piled them up in it. The jewels sparkled and shone so wonderfully that Aladdin's mother was amazed, and agreed to take them to the sultan.

So, next morning, she covered the dish with a fine napkin, carried it to the palace, and presented it to the sultan.

The sultan was in raptures. 'Never, never in my life have I seen such jewels!' he said. 'My good woman, what is the reason for this magnificent gift? Surely you must have some boon to ask in return? Come, tell me what it is!'

'Monarch of monarchs!' said Aladdin's mother. 'Before I tell you, I would be sure of your forgiveness.'

'I will forgive you whatever you may ask!' said the sultan. 'For the gift is so great that the boon can scarcely be greater.'

'Monarch of monarchs, it is my son Aladdin. He has fallen in love with the princess, your daughter. So great is his love that I feared he would die if I did not come and ask you for her hand in marriage. But I pray you to forgive both him and me!'

The sultan turned to his grand vizier. 'What do you say?' he asked. 'Ought I not to bestow my daughter on one who values her at so great a price?'

Now the grand vizier had a son of his own, and he wanted this son to marry the princess. So he begged the sultan to decide nothing for three months. 'By that time,' he said, 'I hope my son will be able to offer your majesty a still more valuable present.'

The sultan, who was greedy for riches, said to Aladdin's mother, 'Good woman, go home and tell your son that I cannot allow my daughter to marry anyone for at least three months. At the end of that time, you may come again.'

Aladdin's mother went home with the news, and Aladdin was overjoyed. He thought about the princess day and night, and marked off every day as it passed as one day nearer to his heart's desire.

But during those days the grand vizier was not idle. He sold his lands, he pawned everything of value he possessed, and in two months' time he was able to go to the sultan with an ivory chest crammed full of gold coins. And since the sultan already had Aladdin's jewels, he thought he might just as well have the grand vizier's gold also, and he agreed that his daughter should marry the vizier's son. But he felt rather ashamed of himself, so he kept the marriage a secret until the very day of the wedding.

On that day Aladdin's mother went out to buy oil, and found the streets crowded with excited people. 'What is going on?' she asked the oil merchant.

'Don't you know?' said he. 'Tonight the princess is to marry the grand vizier's son.'

Aladdin's mother ran home. 'Oh my son,' she cried, 'you are undone! This night the grand vizier's son is to marry the princess!'

Aladdin went to his bedroom, took down the lamp from a shelf, rubbed it, and summoned the genie.

'Master, what is thy will?'

Aladdin said, 'The sultan has broken his word to me. His daughter is this night to be married to the son of the grand vizier. As soon as the wedding feast is over, bring them both here to me.'

'Master, I obey.'

Sure enough, at midnight, the genie appeared again, bringing with him the bed on which the princess and the vizier's son were lying. Were they frightened? Indeed they were!

'Take this newly married man,' said Aladdin. 'Put him outside in the cold, and bring him back at daybreak.'

At once the genie and the vizier's son vanished, and Aladdin was left alone with the princess.

'Don't be afraid,' said Aladdin. 'I'm not going to hurt you. Take your rest. I will keep guard.'

So Aladdin stood at the door of the room till daybreak with a naked sword in his hand. But the princess spent a miserable night.

At daybreak the genie appeared again, carrying the bridegroom on his back.

'Lay him down in the bed,' said Aladdin, 'and carry him and the princess back to the palace.'

Then the bed, the princess, the vizier's son and the genie disappeared. Aladdin laughed. 'So far, so good!'

By and by, at the palace, the sultan went to wish his daughter good morning. The unhappy vizier's son jumped up and ran out of the room. The princess would not say a word. So the sultan went away and sent her mother to her.

Her mother said, 'What is the matter, child, that you will not speak to your father?'

Then the princess wept, and told her mother what had happened. But her mother wouldn't believe it. She said the princess must have been dreaming. But on the next night the same thing happened, and the princess declared it was no dream. The sultan questioned the vizier's son. The vizier's son said the princess was telling the truth. He said, too, that much as he loved the princess, he would rather die than go through such another terrible night. And he begged the sultan to cancel the marriage.

Which the sultan did, to everyone's astonishment.

(v) NEW LAMPS FOR OLD

On the very day that the three months were up, Aladdin sent his mother to the palace to remind the sultan of his promise.

The greedy sultan said, 'Good woman, how do I know that your son is able to support the princess? Tell him he must send me forty gold trays brimful of such jewels as he has already given me, the trays to be carried by forty brown slaves, led by as many handsome young white slaves, all splendidly dressed. If he can do this, he shall marry my daughter.'

So Aladdin rubbed the lamp and bade the genie produce the gold trays and the jewels and the slaves. There were the slaves now, led by Aladdin's mother, marching to the palace in glittering garments, carrying the jewel-filled trays on their heads. They marched into the council chamber, set the trays on the carpet, and after kneeling to the sultan, stood in a half circle round the throne with their hands crossed on their breasts.

'My good woman,' said the delighted sultan to Aladdin's

mother, 'I see that your son is worthy of my daughter. Go, tell him I await him with open arms.'

Aladdin's mother went home with the joyful news. Aladdin again summoned the Slave of the Lamp. 'I want a scented bath,' he said, 'and the richest robe ever worn by a monarch. I want a horse that surpasses the best in the sultan's stables. Give me also twenty slaves to follow me, and twenty more to go before me in two ranks. Besides this, I wish a splendid robe for my mother, and six beautiful slaves to attend her. And lastly I must have twenty purses, each filled with ten thousand pieces of gold.'

No sooner said than done. Aladdin, glowing from the bath, clothed magnificently, and riding a splendid horse, set out for the palace with his mother and his escort of slaves. All the people ran out of their houses to see him pass by; and when the slaves flung the pieces of gold among them, everyone cheered till the streets rang again.

When Aladdin arrived at the palace, the sultan embraced and feasted him. 'You shall marry the princess this very day!' he cried.

But Aladdin said, 'Sire, I would first build a palace worthy to receive your daughter. I pray you grant me a piece of land.'

'Choose what ground you will, and build what you will!' cried the sultan.

So Aladdin went home, summoned the genie, and bade him build a palace. The palace was finished by next day. It was such a palace as had never been seen in the world before, built of gold and silver and gleaming with precious stones. And now Aladdin said he was ready to marry the princess – but only if she were willing.

The princess was willing. The wedding was held amid great rejoicing; and Aladdin and his princess lived happily in their palace for some years.

But far away in Africa the wizard was still hankering after the wonderful lamp. After casting many spells and burning a lot of magic powders, he learned that Aladdin, instead of dying under-ground, had married the princess and was now living in royal splendour. He knew that Aladdin could only have succeeded in doing all this by the help of the lamp, so he spread out his robe and flew till he came to the sultan's city.

Now, unluckily, Aladdin had just set out on an eight days' hunting expedition, so that the wizard had plenty of time. He dis-guised himself as a pedlar, went to a coppersmith and bought a dozen bright copper lamps. With these he hastened to Aladdin's palace, and began walking about under the windows, calling out, 'New lamps for old! New lamps for old!'

A crowd gathered. 'New lamps for old!' mocked the crowd, and pelted the wizard with stones and mud. Much he cared!

The princess heard the uproar and sent a slave to find out what it was all about. The slave came back laughing. 'Madam,' she said, 'there is an old fool outside offering to exchange new lamps for old! Do you think he can possibly mean it?'

The princess laughed also. 'We can soon prove whether he means it or not. There is an old lamp up on the shelf over there. Take it, and see if he will give you a new one for it.'

The slave took the lamp and ran down to the pedlar.

'Give me a new lamp for this!'

The pedlar snatched the lamp. The crowd jeered. The pedlar bade the slave take her choice out of his basket, and when she had done so, he threw the rest of the copper lamps among the crowd, and hurried away.

'Certainly the poor old fellow is mad!' said the slave, carrying the new copper lamp up to the princess.

That night, in a lonely place outside the city gates, the wizard took the wonderful lamp out of the bosom of his robe and rubbed it.

A flash of light, and the genie appeared.

'Master, what is thy will?'

'Take up Aladdin's palace, and the princess and myself, and carry us to Africa,' said the wizard.

Whizz! Off went palace, princess, wizard, lamp and all!

(VI) THE SLAVE OF THE RING

Next morning the sultan looked out of his window to rejoice himself with the sight of Aladdin's palace. What was this? No palace! He sent for the grand vizier and said, 'I have pinched myself, I can't be dreaming! Look out of the window – what do you see?'

The vizier looked out of the window. 'Monarch of monarchs!' he cried. 'I see an empty space where Aladdin's palace should be. That fellow is a rogue – I always knew it! Send for him, bind him, put him to death!'

The sultan sent out his guards. They met Aladdin coming back from the hunt, bound him in chains, and led him to the palace. And the common people, who loved Aladdin, followed him in a great crowd, and pushed their way shouting into the court-yard.

Aladdin stood before the sultan. The sultan wouldn't hear a word from him, but called for the executioner and bade him cut off Aladdin's head. But just as the executioner raised his scimitar, the grand vizier came rushing in, shouting out, 'Stop! Stop! The people have overpowered the guard! They are scaling the walls and breaking down the doors to rescue Aladdin! They are armed, we shall all be murdered!'

So then the sultan was frightened, and sent messengers to the people to say that Aladdin was pardoned.

When Aladdin found himself free, he said to the sultan, 'Sire, I pray you to let me know my crime.'

'Your crime, false wretch!' cried the sultan. 'Follow me and I will show you.' He took Aladdin to a window, and pointed to the

place where his palace had stood. 'Where is your palace!' he cried. 'And where is my daughter?'

Aladdin was too astonished to say anything.

'You have done away with my daughter!' wailed the sultan. 'Is it not just that I should have your head?'

And Aladdin answered, 'Give me but forty days in which to seek her. If I cannot find her, I swear I will return and suffer death at your pleasure. For indeed, without her, my life would not be worth living.'

For three days Aladdin wandered about, seeking the princess, getting no news of her, finding no trace of her. On the fourth day he came to the banks of a river. He was so miserable that he thought he would throw himself in. But flinging up his hands to ask forgiveness of heaven, he caught sight of the ring on his finger.

Well, what a fool he felt, not to have thought of the ring before! He rubbed the ring, there was a flash of light, and the Slave of the Ring stood before him.

'Master, what is thy will?'

'Bring me back my palace and my wife!'

But the Slave of the Ring answered: 'Master, that is not in my power. One genie may not interfere with another's work. You must ask him of the lamp.'

'Then take me where my palace stands,' said Aladdin.

Instantly he found himself in Africa, on the outskirts of a great city. There was his palace before him, and he was standing under the princess's window.

A slave saw him and ran to tell her mistress. The princess opened the window and leaned out. She stretched out her arms to Aladdin, and he stretched up his arms to her. 'Oh my dear, dear love!'

'Hush!' whispered the princess. 'There is a little private door in yonder turret. I have ordered it to be opened. Enter quickly – a slave will lead you to my room.'

Aladdin ran in and bounded up the stairs. There they were now, clasped in each other's arms. 'But tell me quickly, my princess,' said Aladdin, 'what has become of the old lamp which I left on the shelf in my robing room when I went hunting?'

'Alas, alas!' said the princess. 'This trouble is all of my doing!' And she told him how she had given the lamp to the disguised wizard. 'Now he carries it always wrapped in his robe,' she said. 'I know, because he pulled it out and showed it to me in triumph.'

'My princess, we will beat him yet!' said Aladdin. 'I am going into the city. I will come back at noon, and I beg that the private door may be opened to me at my first knock.'

Away went Aladdin. He changed clothes with the first peasant he met, and then walked on into the city and went into a druggist's shop. There he bought a special powder. And after that he went back to the princess, who was herself waiting at the private door, and let him in at his first knock.

'My princess,' said Aladdin, 'put on your most beautiful garments; and when the wizard comes to visit you, receive him with smiles. Let him think you have forgotten me. Invite him to supper, and say that you would like to taste the wine of his country.'

Then Aladdin told the princess what else she must do, and he himself went to hide in a cupboard.

The princess dressed herself in her royal robes; she put on a girdle of emeralds and a crown of diamonds. Then she sent a slave to bid the wizard come to her.

'My lord,' she said, when the wizard came in, 'since all my tears will not bring Aladdin back to me, I have made up my mind to mourn no longer. And so I invite you to sup with me – if such be your pleasure?'

The wizard was amazed and delighted, for up till now the princess had spent her time crying. Now, when she said she would like to taste some of the wine of Africa, he rushed to the cellar to fetch it. Whilst he was gone, the princess put the powder Aladdin had given her into her own cup, and poured wine into the cup. When the wizard came back, she held out the cup to him.

'My lord,' she said, 'will it please you to drink my health in the wine of my country, and I will pledge you in the wine of your country.'

'And so we are reconciled!' said the wizard.

He took the cup of wine from the princess, drained it to the last drop – and fell back lifeless.

The princess ran to the cupboard. Aladdin sprang out. He hurried to the dead wizard, took the lamp from the folds of his robe, and rubbed it.

A flash of light, and the Slave of the Lamp appeared.

'Master, what is thy will?'

'Carry this palace to the place from which you brought it,' said Aladdin.

At once, there they were – princess, Aladdin, palace and all, back in the sultan's city.

The sultan, who had spent the night weeping for his daughter, rose early in the morning and looked out of his window with tear-stained eyes. What did he see? He saw Aladdin's gold and silver palace gleaming in the light of the newly risen sun. Just as he was, in his bed-gown, he rushed over to it. And Aladdin, who had seen him coming, was at the palace gate to welcome him. He brought the sultan to the princess, and told him the whole story. The sultan, weeping now for joy, embraced his daughter many times, and begged Aladdin to forgive him. He proclaimed a ten days' feast for the whole city, and said, 'Now may we all live in peace for the rest of our lives!'

'Yes,' said Aladdin. 'Truly I think this is the end of all our troubles.'

It was the end of all their troubles. Aladdin and his princess lived long and happily. And the Slave of the Lamp and the Slave of the Ring served them faithfully to the end of their days.

7 · Jack and the Wizard

Once upon a time there were two brothers. They had no money; but the elder brother married a rich woman; so then he was rich as well.

The younger brother was called Jack. He went to work for the rich one; but when Jack asked for his wages, his brother said, 'Be off with you!'

'So I will then,' said Jack. And off he went to look for work somewhere else. He travelled a long way. No, no one wanted him.

At sunset he saw a countryman coming along the road. So he stopped this countryman and said, 'What cheer, friend! Can you tell me where I can find work?'

Said the countryman, 'You see that castle over there?'

'If you mean the black one, with the sun going down behind it – yes, I see it.'

Said the countryman, 'That is the Black Enchanted Castle. People who seek work in these parts go there. But a wizard lives in it.'

Said Jack, 'Is he a bad one?'

'Some find him bad, and some find him good,' said the countryman.

Said Jack, 'I'll risk it.'

So he walked on and came to the castle. And there was the wizard, looking out of the door.

The wizard had a round red face and little peeping blue eyes. Said Jack to himself, 'You don't look as if you'd eat me!' So he made bold to ask if the wizard had any work for him.

'Yes, I have work, Jack,' said the wizard. 'To all who come here I give three days' work. And they can't do it, and so I can't pay them.'

'*I* will do it, sir!' said Jack.

The wizard took Jack in, gave him a good supper, and told him to find himself a place to sleep. Jack went upstairs and wandered from room to room. Some rooms were large, some rooms were small, some had grand beds in them, some had hard and narrow ones. Jack didn't choose the largest room, nor the softest bed. But neither did he choose the smallest room and the hardest bed. He chose a middling sized room and a bed neither hard nor soft. And he lay down and slept like a log.

In the morning the wizard gave him a good breakfast. And when Jack had eaten and drunk his fill, the wizard took a small gold watch out of his girdle, and said, 'See this little watch, Jack? I have lost its little key. Your first day's task is to find it for me.'

Off went Jack to search for the little key. He searched all day. He searched the castle through, both inside and outside. Not a blink of a little golden key could he find. So, towards sunset, utterly tired out and nigh heartbroken, he came into the castle yard, where there was a pig trough full of water.

'Bah!' thought he. 'What a task to set a fellow! I won't search any longer!'

And he sat down by the pig trough, and trailed his hand in the water.

Floating on the water was a little twig, about the size of a man's finger. Jack fell to playing with this twig, poking it down under the water, and watching it bob up again. Down, up! Down, up! 'Bah!' thought Jack. 'What a fool I am!' And he took the little twig and broke it in two.

Would you believe it? Out from the little twig, when Jack had broken it, fell the little golden key.

Jack jumped to his feet. Now he wasn't tired, and he wasn't

heartbroken. He ran into the castle, and gave the key to the wizard.

'Good, i'faith, good!' said the wizard. 'Jack, you are the best man that ever came here.'

If the wizard had given Jack a good supper the night before, he gave him a better one this night. And when Jack had eaten his fill, the wizard said, 'Jack, my boy, take the best bed you can find.'

But Jack didn't take the best bed he could find. Only he chose one a little better than the one he had taken the night before. And he lay down, and again slept like a top.

Next morning, after a good breakfast, the wizard said, 'Jack, today you must go a-gardening for me.' And he handed Jack a bundle of coltsfoot plants. 'You'll find a spade outside the back door.'

'And what am I to do with these weeds, master?'

'*Weeds!*' cried the wizard. 'You mustn't say "weeds", Jack. They're magic plants, and so you'll find. Plant them carefully.'

'And where am I to plant them?'

'Anywhere they'll let you,' said the wizard.

Jack took the bundle of coltsfoot, went out, and found a spade at the back door. There was a bed of earth near by, and seeing there was nothing growing on it, Jack turned it over nicely, patted the earth smooth with his two hands, and began to plant. He put in one row of coltsfoot, stamping each plant firmly down with his heel. Then he began on another row. But when he glanced round at the first row – what did he see? Every one of the coltsfoot plants was out of the earth again, with its leaves on the ground and its roots in the air, as if it had turned a somersault.

'Oh well, I'll see to you later,' thought Jack. And he finished planting the second row, and began on the third. But the same thing happened with the second row as had happened with the first. As soon as Jack turned his back on that row, every plant jumped out of the earth and stood on its head.

'Maybe this bit of ground doesn't suit coltsfoot,' thought Jack. And he went and found another piece of ground, and dug it over, and began planting. But the same thing happened. So long as he kept his eye on the plants they stayed in the ground; but immediately he turned his back on them, they somersaulted out of it.

Jack tried another piece of ground, and yet another. He was all day trying, but not a single root of coltsfoot could he get planted. By sunset he was in despair, tired out and heartbroken. He sat down on a stony piece of earth, and thought 'I give up!' He picked up the earth in handfuls and began throwing it about; not for any good it did him, but because he was heartsick. And in one handful of earth he found a dirty old ring.

Jack didn't know whether the ring was gold or silver, or what it was, but he dropped it into his pocket. And directly that ring was in his pocket, a thought came to him. What did he do? He jumped up and began ramming the coltsfoot plants into the earth, leaves down and roots up. He planted one row and began on another; and when he looked over his shoulder at the first row, there were the plants with their roots in the ground and their leaves in the air.

'Oh ho!' thought Jack. 'So that's the way you are! Just plain contrary!'

And he went on planting the way he had begun, roots up, leaves down. He didn't look round at what he had planted, and he didn't look round when he had finished planting. He walked off a step or two, and stood with his back turned, whistling a tune. Then he swung round of a sudden, and looked at the coltsfoot bed. Yes, there they all were, with their broad green leaves shining in the red light of sunset, and their roots still firmly in the ground.

So Jack went into the castle, and told the wizard he had finished his task.

The wizard said, 'I must come and look.'

He went and looked. 'Good, i'faith, good! Jack, you are the lad for me!'

And that evening he stuffed Jack up with such good meat and drink that, after he had eaten, Jack went upstairs and tumbled into the first bed he came to – whether best or worst he didn't know nor care, though the wizard had bidden him take the best one.

In the morning, after a breakfast such as Jack had never had in his life before, the wizard said, 'Today, Jack, you must find *me*.' And when he had said that, he vanished.

Oh dear! Jack ran up and down inside the castle, and he ran up and down outside the castle, looked here, looked there, looked everywhere. He searched till sunset; he grew cross and weary and heartbroken.

Said he, 'What a senseless task! How can I find a man who vanishes? A thousand times better to look for a needle in a haystack, because at least the needle *is* in the haystack, and if you search long enough you're bound to find it. But this old fellow, he may be at my elbow, laughing at me, for all I know – or care! I give up!'

And he went into a stable, and sat down to rest in a corner.

In the corner was a bundle of straw. Jack picked up a handful of straw for no reason at all, and found an egg. 'I'll suck this egg,' thought he, 'for I doubt if I'll get any supper tonight.' He picked up a pebble to crack the top of the egg: and when he cracked the egg – out jumped the wizard!

'Good, i' faith, good! Jack, if there's a smarter lad than you in the world, I'd like to meet him!'

So they went back into the castle, and Jack got a supper fit for a king. And being told to take the best bed in the castle, that night he took it, and went to sleep well pleased with himself.

Next morning the wizard said, 'Jack, you are the first lad ever I found who has managed to get through the three tasks I set. Your time is up, and you may go home. Now then – your wages. Which will you have, one gold coin with my blessing, or a hatful of gold coins with my cursing?'

Said Jack, 'I will have no man's cursing, let alone the cursing of a man such as you. Give me the one gold coin.'

'Good, i' faith, good!' said the wizard. He gave Jack the one gold coin, and Jack went home.

Jack lived on that gold coin for a week or two; and when he had nothing left, he thought he would go off again and look for work. Then he remembered the old ring he had picked up in the wizard's garden, and thought perhaps he might sell it.

He took the ring out of his pocket: it was tarnished and covered with earth. So he got a cloth and began to rub it clean, to see whether it was gold or silver or just some common metal. And when he rubbed it – what do you think? A most beautiful maiden stood before him.

'What do you ask of me?' she said.

But Jack just gaped at her and said nothing. He was too surprised.

'I am the maiden of the Black Enchanted Castle,' said she, 'and that is my ring you found. Whatever you ask, I will grant you.'

'Faith, lady,' said Jack, 'I am a poor man and my cupboard is bare. I should like something to eat.'

The maiden waved her hand over Jack's table. And the table immediately covered itself with meat and drink. Then she waved her hand over Jack's cupboard. 'You will find your cupboard well stocked,' she said.

And then she nodded to him, and disappeared.

Jack had food for several days; but the day came when his cupboard was bare again. He wondered whether the maiden of the Black Enchanted Castle would bring him more food if he summoned her. He took the ring out of his pocket and gave it a little tap. But the maiden did not come. Then he thought again, and fetched a cloth, and rubbed the ring. And there was the maiden.

She was smiling, and she looked lovelier than before. 'What do you ask of me this time?' she said.

'Lady,' said Jack, 'if it's all the same to you, I should like some more food.'

The maiden waved her hand, and the food appeared.

'Is that all?' she said. 'Think again, Jack!'

Jack thought; he looked round at his poor little one-roomed cottage, with its damp walls and its earth floor. Maybe the maiden put the idea into his head, but it suddenly seemed to Jack that the place wasn't fit for a pig to live in; and much less fit for such a lovely maiden to visit.

'I should like to be living in a beautiful little mansion,' he said, 'fit for the likes of you to appear in.'

What do you think now? No sooner were the words out of his mouth, than Jack's poor little cottage disappeared. There he was, standing in the prettiest little mansion you can picture. A gem of a house, both inside and out, not too big, not too small; with servants in the kitchen, and fires blazing brightly in all the rooms, and pictures on the walls, and books on the shelves, and gardens bright with flowers, and stables with sleek shining horses rattling their halter chains, and a dairy with pans of cream and tubs of butter, and cows in one meadow, and sheep in another. Well, well, well, it was days before Jack had done admiring it all, and got used to giving orders to his servants, and having those orders carried out.

And then, one morning, he heaved a great sigh, and rubbed the ring again.

There was the maiden, lovelier than ever, and she was laughing.

'What do you ask of me, Jack?' she said.

'Lady,' said Jack, 'I am very lonely. Could you find it in your heart to live here with me?'

The maiden laughed most merrily. 'That is just what I have been waiting for, Jack,' she said.

84

So they were married next day. And the ring Jack put on the maiden's finger was the ring he had found in the wizard's garden. The wizard came to the wedding. Said he, 'Good, i' faith, good! Now, Jack, you have my daughter and my blessing. May you both live long and happily!'

And they did.

8 · The Silver Penny

A young soldier called Marzi was going home after the wars, and singing as he went: 'My good little father, my good little mother, my dear little home, now I shall see you all once more!'

But when he got home he found that his parents were dead, and their goods had been divided up among his brothers.

Said Marzi, 'Is there nothing left for me?'

Said his eldest brother, 'You! We thought you had been killed off long ago. There is nothing left but a silver penny. You're welcome to that.'

So Marzi took the silver penny, turned his back on his home, and set out into the wide world to seek his fortune.

He went and he went, up hill and down dale, till he came to a wood. In the wood an old man dressed in rags came hobbling towards him.

'Alms, alms, my merry young sir!' cried the old man. 'Alms to buy me a crust of bread and a night's lodging!'

Marzi put his hand in his pocket and pulled out the silver penny. 'If I had more you should have more,' he said, 'but this is all I have. Take it and welcome.'

What was his surprise when the old beggar disappeared! There in his place stood a king of a man, wearing a cloak of oak leaves.

'I am the Wizard of the Wood,' said this king of a man, 'and to all who do good I do good. Ask what you will, and your wish shall be granted.'

Marzi thought a while. Then he said, 'I have often wondered

how it would feel to be something quite different from myself.
God's creatures – bless them! – the beasts of the field, and the
birds of the air, and the fish of the sea, must look upon the world
with other eyes than mine. So, if it is not too much to ask, I would
like the power of changing myself at will into a hare, a dove, and a
salmon.'

'Your wish is granted,' said the Wizard of the Wood. 'Go your
way, and sometimes think of me.'

When he had said that, the wizard vanished. Marzi walked on. When he came to a meadow, he changed himself into a hare. The hare nibbled the grass and skipped from tussock to tussock. 'How good life is, how good!' said the little hare.

The hare became Marzi again and Marzi walked on. When he came to some trees, he changed himself into a dove, and flew up among the branches. 'Coo, coo,' said the little dove. 'Here I will build my nest and find my love. How happy I am, how happy!'

The dove became Marzi again and Marzi walked on. When he came to a river, he changed himself into a silver salmon. The salmon swam in the cool, clear water. 'There is no life so joyous and free as my life!' said the salmon.

The salmon became Marzi again and Marzi walked on; he walked out of his own country and into another one. At sunset he came to a big city. The streets were crowded with people, dancing and singing. And among the people were recruiting sergeants in glittering uniforms, calling out, 'Our king is going to the wars! Our king has need of brave soldiers! Who will enlist in the king's army, and win for himself a glorious name?'

'I will enlist,' said Marzi. 'I have been a soldier, and I will fight in any good cause.'

Now Marzi was a splendid-looking young fellow, tall and strong and handsome. And he knew all that a soldier should know. So he was chosen to be one of the king's bodyguard, and that was a great honour.

Off they marched to the war, and the soldiers said to Marzi, 'However powerful the enemy, we are bound to be victorious. Our king has never been beaten yet. He possesses a magic ring, and so long as that ring is on his finger, he is invincible.'

So they marched and they marched, a long, long way, in high good spirits.

But alack the day! When they came to the field of battle, the enemy was too strong for them; and fight as valiantly as they

88

might, they were all but defeated. The bewildered king ordered a retreat. He looked down at his finger, 'Heaven help me!' he cried. 'I have left my magic ring at home! The man who fetches me my ring before we are overpowered by the enemy shall have the hand of my only daughter as a reward!'

But the danger was immediate, and the king's capital was a long way off. It would take the swiftest rider seven days and seven nights to cross all the rivers, mountains and plains that stretched between the battlefield and the king's palace. The soldiers said, 'We will fight bravely, and die if we must! It is impossible to get that ring in time.'

But Marzi, remembering the wizard's magic gifts, went to the king and said, 'I will bring the ring, your majesty. And when I have brought it, I pray you to remember your promise.'

In a moment he had changed himself into a hare, and was running from the camp so swiftly that the dust rose about him in clouds. One soldier, who was jealous of Marzi, because Marzi was in the king's bodyguard and he was not, threw a stone at the hare. 'I always knew there was something wrong about that fellow!' he muttered to himself.

But the stone hit the ground and bounded back and struck the jealous soldier on the cheek, which didn't make him like Marzi any better.

Along the plain and up hill and down dale raced the little hare, faster than hare had ever raced before. When he came to a river, he changed himself into a silver salmon and swam across. When he came to the mountains, he changed himself into a dove and sped through the air over their rocky tops. The dove came at last to the king's city. There it saw the princess sitting at an open window; it flew in through the window and perched upon her knee.

'Oh you pretty thing!' cried the princess. 'Come, I will fetch you some milk and sugar!'

But the dove shook its feathers violently and fluttered from her knee. There was Marzi now in his own shape, standing before the astonished princess. If she had been pleased with the dove, she was a thousand times more pleased with Marzi.

She heard his story, and fetched the king's ring for him. 'Take it,' she said. 'And when my father comes back victorious, you will be my husband! Oh my brave, handsome Marzi, how happy we shall be! But beware of jealousy, my Marzi. There may be those who will envy you.'

'Since that is possible,' said Marzi, 'I pray you, my princess, to keep three tokens of me to show to the king.' Then he changed himself into a dove, perched on the princess's knee and said, 'Now pluck a feather from each of my wings.'

The princess plucked out the two feathers. The dove changed itself into a salmon. Said the salmon, 'Now scrape off eight of my silver scales.'

The princess scraped off the eight scales. The salmon changed itself into a hare. Said the hare, 'Now cut off my little tail.'

The princess did not want to cut off the hare's tail. She cried a little. But the hare said, 'Hurry! Hurry! There is no time to lose!' So she took her scissors, and *snip* – the tail was off.

The princess put the two feathers and the eight silver scales and the hare's tail into a little golden box. The hare changed itself into a dove, took the king's ring in its beak, and flew out of the window.

The dove flew and flew, over the mountains, over the great river, across the plain. But when it drew near to the king's camp, a violent wind arose, and blew upon the poor little thing so fiercely that it could make no headway. So it changed itself into a hare. The hare took the ring between its teeth, and sped on.

Now the jealous soldier who had seen Marzi gallop away in the shape of a hare, was watching for him to come back. He hid himself behind a bush, and when he saw the little hare speeding towards him, he raised his gun and shot it. There was the poor little hare now, lying dead in the dust. The jealous soldier took the ring from between its teeth, and hurried to the king.

'Behold, I have brought you your ring, oh king!'

The king was overjoyed. 'My brave soldier, it is you and none other who shall wed my daughter!' he cried.

The king put the ring on his finger, and summoned his army to advance and renew the battle. This time they were victorious. The enemy were routed, and their country conquered. The king set off for home, carrying with him an immense amount of treasure and thousands of prisoners.

When the king came to his palace, the princess ran out to greet him . . . But where was Marzi, her hero, the man she loved?

The king took the jealous soldier by the hand. 'My daughter,' he said, 'here is the man to whom we owe our glorious victory. I have promised him your hand in marriage. Tomorrow we will hold a feast in honour of our conquest, and at the same time we will celebrate your wedding.'

The princess burst into tears and ran back into the palace. She cried and cried all day and all night. She wouldn't eat, she couldn't sleep, she made herself ill with crying. She became so ill that the wedding had to be put off; and still she sat and cried.

The king was worried nigh out of his wits. He summoned all his doctors. The princess wouldn't speak to them; she went on crying. The doctors said, 'We cannot find what ails her. She won't speak to us, or take our medicines – there is nothing we can do.'

And all this time the poor little hare was lying stiff and cold on the dusty plain behind the deserted camp. But the Wizard of the Wood had not forgotten him. The wizard looked in his magic mirror and saw the hare lying in the dust. And swifter than the wind blows, he flew to his side. He stooped and blew into the hare's nostrils. 'Hare, little hare, get up and live! Speed to the king's palace! Another stands in your place!'

The hare sprang up alive and well. When he came to the river he changed himself into a silver salmon and swam across. Then he changed himself into a dove, flew up over the mountains, came down at the king's palace, flew in through a window, fluttered his wings, and changed into Marzi.

Here was Marzi now, standing before the king.

'I have come to remind you of your promise, O king!'

The king frowned. 'My promise – what do you mean?'

'It was I who fetched you your magic ring,' said Marzi.

But of course the king didn't believe him. He said Marzi was an imposter and deserved to be hanged.

'I am no imposter,' said Marzi. 'Take me to the princess. You shall hear from her own lips who is her rightful bridegroom – I or that deceiver over there!'

The king didn't know what to think. When he looked closely at Marzi he recognized him as the man who had offered to fetch the ring; but then – the other man had brought it.

'Very well, you shall be taken to the princess,' he said.

The princess was still crying. She had her face hidden in her hands. 'Daughter,' said the king, 'look up.'

But the princess wouldn't look up. She went on crying.

'My princess,' whispered Marzi.

The princess sprang up. She ran to Marzi and flung her arms round his neck. 'Here is my bridegroom,' she cried. 'It was to this man I gave the ring!'

But the king said, 'This is extraordinary! He is certainly not the man who gave the ring to me! How can I decide between them!'

'*I* can decide between them!' said the princess.

She fetched the little golden box in which she had put Marzi's three tokens. She took her seat on a golden chair – she was every inch a princess! 'My bridegroom is the one who can change himself into a dove, a salmon and a hare.' She turned to the false bridegroom. 'Come, let me see *you* do that!' she said scornfully.

But the false bridegroom stood motionless.

'And you?' said the princess to Marzi.

Immediately Marzi vanished, and a white dove flew on to the princess's lap.

'Princess dear,' cooed the dove. 'I lack a feather from each wing.'

The princess took two white feathers from the golden box, and laid one on each of the dove's wings. The dove fluttered its wings: the feathers did not drop.

'You see,' said the princess to the king. 'The feathers are growing where they belong.'

'This is more than extraordinary!' gasped the king.

Then the dove disappeared, and a silver salmon lay on the princess's lap. 'My princess,' said the salmon, 'give me back my eight silver scales.'

The princess took the eight silver scales out of the golden box, and put them back in their places.

'You see?' she said to the king.

The king merely nodded. He was too astonished to speak.

Then the salmon disappeared, and a tailless hare stood at the princess's feet.

'My princess whom I love,' said the hare, 'give me back my little tail.'

The princess took the hare's little tail out of the golden box. 'Turn round, my hare, that I may put it back,' she said.

The hare turned round. The princess set the little tail in its place. 'You see,' she said to the king, 'it grows where it belongs.'

The hare disappeared, and Marzi stood before the king. 'I became a hare, I became a salmon, I became a dove,' he said. 'I sped over the dusty plain, across the broad river, over the high mountains. I reached the palace, I fetched the ring, I sped back with it. But when I neared the camp, that false one over there shot me and stole the ring. Is it I who have won the princess, or is it that cringing thief?'

'It is you,' said the king. He turned to the false bridegroom. 'Be off, rogue, out of my kingdom! If ever you come into my sight again, I will hang you from the nearest gallows!'

The false bridegroom fled. The princess and Marzi were married that very day. The king presented the kingdom he had conquered to Marzi. And in that kingdom Marzi and his queen lived and reigned long and happily.

9 · Kojata

Once upon a time, and a long time ago, there was a king whose beard reached down to his knees. This king was a good king; he ruled over a rich country, and he had a loving wife, but he had no children, and that grieved him. So one day he thought, 'I must not stay here in my palace grieving for the children I have not got. I must think about other things. I will set out and travel through my kingdom to see how my people are getting on.'

The king set out with a retinue of horses and servants. He travelled for several months, and everywhere his people received him with joy, for he was well loved. Then, having visited every part of his kingdom, he and his servants turned homeward again. And as they journeyed, the sun blazed down on them, and the dust flew up.

By and by they came to a place of grass and trees. The king said to his servants, 'We are hot and weary; we will travel no farther until the cool of the evening. Pitch the tents here on the grass, and when that is done, you may all lie down and rest.'

The servants pitched the tents; then they lay down under the trees, and fell asleep.

And the king was seized with a great thirst. He looked round for water, but found none. He looked at his sleeping servants and thought, 'Poor things, I will not wake them, I will go in search of water myself.'

So he got on his horse, and rode off to look for a spring.

He hadn't ridden far when he came to a well: the well was full

to the brim with clear water, and on the water a golden goblet was floating. 'Ah!' The king got off his horse, stooped over the well, and stretched out his hand to lift the goblet.

But the goblet bounced away from his hand; it bobbed down under the water, and came up on the opposite side of the well. The king went round the well, stooped, made a grab at the goblet – again that goblet bobbed away from him. Now it was back where he had first seen it.

Again the king went round the well, again he stooped and tried to lay hold of the goblet, again it bobbed away. He tried to grasp it with one hand, he tried to grasp it with both hands – all no good. The goblet was like a live thing – the king couldn't catch it.

And his thirst grew greater and greater.

'Bah!' thought he. 'I can quench my thirst without a cup!' He lay flat, he put his lips and chin into the water, he drank and drank – and his long beard streamed down into the well.

'Ah! how good it is to drink! How good!'

When he could drink no more, he thought to get up and go back to the tents. But what was this? He couldn't lift his head! Someone was holding his long beard fast under the water.

'Who's there? Let me go!'

No answer – not a sound! Only, grinning up at him from the depths of the well, a face with blazing green eyes and a mouth that stretched from ear to ear: a huge man with claws where his hands should be; and those claws were clinging to the king's beard.

'Let me go! Let me go!'

The king struggled and tugged; he beat at the claws with his hands, he nearly tumbled head first into the well. No good: the claws held fast. And then at last the sound of a hoarse voice came bubbling up through the water.

'I am the wizard, Kojata. You have drunk of my well without my leave. I will never let you go unless you make me a promise.'

'What promise?'

'A promise to give me the most precious thing your palace contains; the precious thing that was not there when you came away.'

It didn't take the king long to give that promise! The only thing in his palace that he held precious was the queen and she was assuredly there when he came away. As for any other precious thing that might have been brought into the palace in his absence – were it ring or jewel or costly ornament – well, the wizard was welcome to it!

'Yes, I promise to give it to you – whatever it is,' said the king.

'Agreed!' The claws let go their hold; the grinning face disappeared in the depths of the well. The king scrambled to his feet, wrung the water out of his beard, and rode back to the tents.

In the cool of the evening, the king's servants woke and packed up the tents; and the cavalcade rode off on their way home. When the king reached his capital he heard the firing of welcoming guns. All the streets were hung with banners and strewn with flowers, and the people ran out of their houses to greet him with shouts and cheers. The king smiled. 'How my people love me!' he thought.

So they did love him; but that day they rejoiced for a special reason; and the king did not yet know that reason.

The cheering crowd brought the king to the palace. What did he see then? He saw his queen being carried towards him in a litter, and beside the queen walked his chief minister, with a golden cushion in his arms. And on the cushion lay a day-old baby – a little prince, very lovely.

Now the king knew what precious thing it was that he had promised to the wizard Kojata. Ah me! Ah me! He took his baby son in his arms and burst into tears . . . The people cheered more loudly than ever, for they thought he was weeping for joy.

The king told no one of his promise. Year followed year. The baby prince, whom they christened Alexey, grew up into a handsome youth. No one came to claim him. And, in time, what had happened at the well became to the king like the memory of a bad dream. He pushed the memory from him, and concerned himself with governing well and wisely.

One day, with a merry party, prince Alexey rode out to hunt. He chased a wild boar and he galloped so fast that he outdistanced his companions. Now he was alone in a dark wood. He rode on through the wood and came to an open space, all overgrown with thistles. In the middle of this space was a lime tree.

The prince looked at the tree. 'I don't remember having seen this before!' he thought.

Then the trunk of the tree opened, and out of it stepped a big man with green eyes and a green chin.

'A fine day, Prince Alexey!' said the green-eyed man. 'You have kept me waiting for long enough!'

'But in the name of wonder – who are you?' said the prince.

'You will know soon enough,' said the green-eyed man. 'Go home and greet your father from me. Remind him of his debt, and tell him I await its payment.'

Then the green-eyed man went back into the tree. The prince rode home and said to his father, 'Something extraordinary has happened! A man with green eyes came out of a tree. He bade me remind you of the debt you owe him.'

'Oh my son, my son!' wailed the king. 'Oh my accursed beard! What sorrow it has brought upon us! I will send for the barber and have it cut off this very moment!'

The prince felt more bewildered than ever. What could his father's beard have to do with a green-eyed man who came out of a tree? But whilst waiting for the barber, the weeping king told the prince of all that had happened at the well.

Then the prince said, 'Father, a promise is a promise, and must be kept; a debt is a debt and must be paid. Give me a good horse and your blessing for my journey, and I will be off. Keep hope in your heart! For I think that sooner or later I shall come back to you.'

The king gave the prince the best horse in his stable; he gave him a saddle of red leather, and a bridle and stirrups of gold. He gave him also a sharp sword, with a diamond hilt and a jewelled scabbard. The queen hung a little cross round the prince's neck; and when they had both blessed him and wept over him, Prince Alexey rode away.

He went first to the place where he had seen the lime tree, but the tree was no longer there. So he rode straight on, not knowing where he must go. He rode for two days, and on the third day he came to a lake in a green valley. On the lake thirty brightly coloured ducks were swimming; and on the shore thirty little white shifts were spread out in the sun.

The prince got off his horse and went to look at the little white shifts. He picked one up: it was soft as silk and light as gossamer. He looked at the ducks, he looked at the shifts. 'Something mysterious here!' he thought. And still keeping the one little shift in his hand, he hid himself among some bulrushes.

The ducks swam and sported; they dived down deep, came up, swam around. By and by they came paddling to shore. Twenty-nine of them picked up their little white shifts, put them on, and turned into twenty-nine beautiful maidens. One moment those maidens stood on the shore; the next moment the earth opened and they vanished.

But the thirtieth little duck ran about searching: it could not find its little shift; it cried piteously, and went back into the water. It was still crying piteously, stretching up its little neck, and turning its little head from side to side.

Then it caught sight of the prince crouched among the bulrushes, and called out, 'Oh prince, prince, prince, for pity's sake, give me back my little shift!'

The prince came out from the bulrushes and laid the shift on the bank.

The duck flew to put it on. Now there she stood, no longer a duck but a most beautiful maiden. The maiden held out her hand and smiled.

'You are Prince Alexey,' she said, 'and I am Princess Nadya, the youngest daughter of the wizard Kojata, whose kingdom is underground. My father has long waited for your coming; and his rage is terrible. Now you must come with me and do exactly as I tell you. As soon as you see my father you must at once throw yourself on the ground, and approach him on your knees. He will stamp and roar and curse, but you must draw near to him boldly; and above all, show no fear. Take my hand and we will go to him.'

Holding Alexey's hand, the princess struck her foot sharply on the ground. The earth opened and they sank down into a lower world.

There stood Kojata's palace, hewn out of a single ruby, and glowing with red light. In the centre of a great hall, lit by glittering diamonds, the wizard sat on a golden throne with a sparkling crown on his head. His green eyes flashed fire, his mouth stretched from ear to ear, and instead of hands he had claws. As soon as he saw the prince he began to stamp and curse, and uttered such piercing yells that the whole palace shook.

The prince flung himself on his knees. Was he afraid? Perhaps he was; but he remembered what the Princess Nadya had told him, and at least he showed no signs of fear. Still on his knees he crawled slowly forward towards the throne. He looked absurd. When he had nearly reached the throne, the wizard's angry yells changed into shouts of laughter.

'You young rogue! It is well for you that you have made me laugh! Come, we will be friends! Welcome to the underworld! All the same, because of your delay in coming here, I shall impose three tasks upon you. That will be tomorrow. Tonight you may eat and sleep.'

Then two pages in flame-coloured livery led Prince Alexey away to a splendid room and served him with supper. And after he had eaten, Alexey lay down on the soft bed that had been prepared for him, and slept soundly.

Early next morning the wizard sent for him. Said he, 'Now let us see how clever you are! By this time tomorrow you must build me a marble palace, with windows of crystal and a roof of gold. The palace is to stand in the middle of a beautiful garden with fish ponds and waterfalls. If you are able to do this, we shall be friends. If you are not able to do it – off goes your head, for I have no use for people who are not clever.'

Prince Alexey went sadly to his room. He sat on his bed and thought, 'Tomorrow I must die!' He did not stir all day, and when the pages brought him food, he could not eat it.

In the evening he heard a tapping at the window, and a little voice said, 'Open! Open!' He opened the window and a bee flew in. The bee alighted on the ground, and changed into the Princess Nadya.

'Prince Alexey, why are you sad?'

'How should I not be sad? Your father has set me an impossible task, and tomorrow I must die.'

'No, you shall not die,' said the princess. 'I will build the palace for you. Sleep in peace tonight, and tomorrow when you wake the palace will be finished.'

It turned out just as the princess had said. When Alexey woke in the morning – there was the marble palace, with windows of crystal and roof of gold, standing in a beautiful garden, all complete with fish ponds and waterfalls.

Prince Alexey clapped his hands. 'No, I shall not die today,' he thought.

Then the wizard came. He could find no fault with the palace.

He said, 'I see you are clever with your hands. Now let us see if you have also a clever brain. I have thirty daughters, all beautiful. Tomorrow I shall place them in a row. You shall walk past them three times, and the third time you must tell me which is my youngest daughter. If you can tell me, we shall be friends. If you cannot tell me – off goes your head. For I have no use for people without brains.'

Prince Alexey went away laughing. Not recognize the princess Nadya? How should he fail to recognize her, when he loved her with all his heart? He spent a happy day, and in the evening, when he went to his room, he was looking forward to his tomorrow's task.

'How absurdly easy!' he thought. And he laughed aloud.

Then he heard a tapping at the window, and a little voice said, 'Open! Open!' He opened the window, a bee flew in, and changed into the Princess Nadya.

'Prince Alexey, why are you laughing?'

'How should I not laugh, my beautiful one, at the task your father has set me? When I cannot tell the difference between you and every other woman in the world, then it will be time for my heart to stop beating!'

'Gallant words, my prince, but rash ones! My twenty-nine sisters and I are so exactly alike that even my father, were it not for his magic, could not tell us apart.'

'I do not believe it!' he said.

'You must believe it!' she said. 'For it is true. Listen to me, Alexey – your life depends on what I am going to tell you. When my sisters and I stand before you, you will know me by a ladybird on my left eyelid. Look very carefully, and take your time, you might easily overlook so small a thing.'

When she had said that, the princess changed into a bee again, and flew out of the window. And the prince went to bed.

In the morning the wizard sent for him. The wizard was sitting on his throne in the great hall, and opposite him in a long line stood thirty maidens. The maidens were dressed in white, their eyes were bent on the ground, their hands were clasped in front of them, they were still as statues. And – heaven help us! – they were all so exactly alike that it seemed to prince Alexey as if they must be but one maiden reflected in twenty-nine mirrors.

The wizard was grinning from ear to ear. 'Ah ha!' said he, 'I've puzzled you this time! Now my clever prince, you may look at them all once, you may look at them all twice, you may look at them all three times; and after that, unless you can tell me which is the youngest – off goes your head!'

Prince Alexey walked past that line of maidens once; he walked past them a second time: he walked very slowly, peering up into each face to see if anyone had a ladybird on the left eyelid. He could not find that ladybird – what was he to do? He felt desperate, but he said to himself, 'Third time lucky!' and began slowly, slowly to walk down the line of maidens for the last time. And then, when he reached the nineteenth maiden, his heart gave a bound. There was the tiny ladybird, the merest speck of a thing, on the maiden's left eyelid. He seized the maiden's hand. 'This is your youngest daughter!' he cried joyfully.

The wizard Kojata gave a yell that shook the palace. 'There is some jugglery here!' he shouted. 'I won't have it! Someone is helping you! But you shall not escape me so easily. I have yet a third task for you. In three hours from now I shall set alight a handful of straw, and before that straw is burnt up you shall turn it into a pair of boots. You shall do this in my presence, you rogue, that I may see with my own eyes if anyone helps you!'

The prince went to his room. He was in despair. He heard the little voice at the window crying 'Open, open!' He opened the window, in flew the bee and changed into princess Nadya.

'I do not ask why you are sad, my prince,' she said. 'Alas, alas, this time my father has made sure that I shall not help you!'

'Then I must die,' said Alexey. 'But oh my beautiful one, it will be hard to leave you!'

And the princess answered, 'You shall not leave me. We will live together, or die together.'

She went to the window and breathed on it, and her breath froze on the pane. Then she took the prince by the hand and led him out of the room. She locked the door and threw away the key. Hand in hand they ran out of the palace. They ran till they came to the spot where they had first arrived in the lower world. There the princess lifted up her eyes and whispered a magic word. The dome of the lower world opened, and the prince and princess rose up and up until they stood on the green earth, in the sunlight by the side of the lake. The prince's horse was still grazing there. The moment he saw his master, the horse whinnied and galloped towards him. Prince Alexey sprang into the saddle, swung the princess up behind him, and away they went, like an arrow from a bow.

But in his palace in the underworld, the wizard Kojata was counting the hours. When the three hours had passed, he ordered his servants to bring in a handful of straw and lay it at his feet. And when they had done that, he bade them summon Prince Alexey. The servants went to the prince's room, found the door locked, and knocked on it.

And the frozen breath on the window-pane spoke in Alexey's voice, and said, 'I am coming directly.'

The servants went back to the wizard. The wizard was stamping with impatience. He waited but five minutes. Then he sent his servants again to summon the prince.

The servants knocked at the door. The breath on the pane answered, 'I am coming directly.' And the servants went back to the wizard. The wizard, stamping furiously, waited another five minutes. Then he sent his servants again. Again they knocked; again came the answer, 'I am coming directly.'

The servants went back to the wizard. He yelled with rage and clashed his claws together. 'The young knave is making a mock of me!' he shrieked. 'Break open the door!'

The servants broke open the door. Nobody inside! Only the frozen breath on the pane in fits of laughter.

The servants went to tell the wizard. His rage was terrible. He ordered out his soldiers.

'Pursue Prince Alexey!' he shouted. 'Catch him and bring him back to me. If you do not catch him – your heads shall pay for it!'

The prince and princess were galloping, galloping. They had a good start and they were laughing, thinking their troubles were over. But suddenly the princess said, 'Hush! Listen! Do you hear anything behind us?'

The prince sprang from the saddle and put his ear to the ground. 'Yes, I hear the sound of galloping hoofs!'

'Then there is no time to lose,' said the princess. And she turned herself into a river, the prince into an iron bridge, and the horse into a blackbird. Beyond the river the road branched off into three ways.

The wizard's soldiers came galloping, galloping. They crossed the iron bridge, and then they drew rein. There were the three ways – which way should they go? They dismounted and searched for hoof marks: there were none. They mounted again and galloped a little way down one road, down another. They came back to the bridge in despair. In terror of their lives they went back and told the wizard.

'Fools! Imbeciles!' shrieked the wizard. 'The bridge was the prince, the river the princess! Go back at once and bring them here, or your heads shall pay for it!'

The soldiers set out again. Alexey and the princess were galloping, galloping. They looked round. There were the soldiers close behind them! Immediately the princess changed herself and the prince and his horse into a huge forest, where a thousand paths and roads crossed and recrossed each other.

'They went this way!' cried the soldiers, and dashed into the forest. They galloped this way and that way: they found nothing but the crowding trees and the maze of roads that turned and twisted and brought them back to where they had started. In terror of their lives they went back and told the wizard.

'A horse! A horse!' shrieked the wizard. 'I will go after them myself!'

The wizard was galloping, galloping: the prince and princess were galloping. They heard the sound of hoofs behind them. 'That is my father himself!' said the princess. 'But his power only reaches as far as the first church. Give me your cross.'

Prince Alexey handed her the cross that his mother had hung round his neck. The princess held it in her hand. She changed herself into a church, the prince into a monk, and the horse into a wax candle.

The wizard rode up to the church and said to the monk, 'Have you seen two travellers on horseback pass this way?'

'Yes,' said the monk. 'Prince Alexey and the daughter of the wizard Kojata have just gone by. They stopped but a few moments to enter the church and say their prayers. They bade me light this wax candle for you, and give you their greeting.'

Then at last the wizard knew that he was beaten, for his power did not reach beyond the church. He rode home to his underworld kingdom, ordered his soldiers to be lined up before him, and sent for the executioner.

'Off with their heads!' he screamed.

But the executioner said, 'Think what you are about. You cannot do without your soldiers!'

The wizard knew that the executioner spoke truth. So he swallowed his rage and dismissed his soldiers.

Meanwhile the prince and princess were galloping on their way.

What rejoicing when they arrived at the king's city! Bells rang out, the people cheered and shouted, the king and queen laughed and wept. The prince and princess were married. The king looked at his lovely daughter-in-law, and said, 'In the beginning my beard caused us to live in trouble, so I cut it off. But in the end, behold it has caused us to live in happiness! I will grow it again!'

So he grew his beard again, and it soon reached down to his knees.

10 · Rich Woman, Poor Woman

Once upon a time there lived a mighty wizard. You may be sure that everyone treated him with great respect. But one day he thought to himself, 'This is all very well: people flatter me for what I can give them – how do I know what they are really like?'

So he put on a dirty old cloak, took a crutch under his arm, and hobbled out in the guise of a lame beggar.

All day he hobbled from village to village. He met with some kindness and some unkindness; and in the evening he came to the door of a big house. Smoke was rising from the kitchen chimney, and there was a smell of cooking.

The wizard sniffed. 'What a delicious smell! They are making pancakes in there. Perhaps they will give me one – I feel very hungry.'

So he knocked at the door.

Nobody came. He knocked again. Nobody came. He knocked a third time. The door was flung open, and the mistress of the house peered out. She was richly dressed, and looked very stout and important.

'What do you want?'

'I have been walking all day,' said the wizard. 'I am very hungry. Perhaps of your kindness you would spare me a morsel to eat? Your pancakes smell delicious!'

'They are not for beggars,' said the rich woman. 'Go away!'

'Could you give me perhaps a crust of bread?' said the wizard.

'I will give you nothing,' said the rich woman. 'Go away, before I set the dog on you!'

And she slammed the door in his face.

The wizard hobbled on. It was getting dark when he came to a poor little hut. He went to the door and knocked. The door was opened at once. A woman with a thin pale face looked out.

'I was wondering,' said the wizard, 'if you had a crust of bread to spare? I have walked a long way, and I am very hungry.'

'Why yes,' said the woman. 'Come in! You are welcome to anything I have.'

She brought him into a little kitchen where six small children were playing before a fire of furze wood.

The wizard smiled at the children. 'You have your hands full, ma'am!'

'Why yes,' said the woman. 'I suppose I have . . . There are potatoes boiling in the pot, and there's a loaf of bread and some goats' milk cheese. Poor fare, but it's all I can offer you.'

'You are a widow, ma'am?'

The woman's eyes filled with tears. 'My husband died last week,' she said. 'He was a weaver – oh, such a good man! But all he has left us is a piece of cloth he was weaving before he died. Tomorrow I shall spread out the cloth and measure it. And when I know what length it is, I shall take it to the town and sell it . . . But come, draw up your chair to the table, and eat. For myself, if you'll excuse me, I don't feel hungry.'

The woman said this because she knew there was not enough food to go round. But when she set the food on the table, to her astonishment she found that there was plenty and to spare for the children and for the lame beggar and for herself.

Yes, she was astonished. But she said nothing.

Whilst she put the children to bed, the wizard sat by the fire and kept it blazing. He was taking furze sticks from the wood pile and tossing them into the flames; and the more furze he tossed into the fire, the bigger grew the wood pile.

Again the woman was astonished. And again she said nothing.

After a while, the wizard got up to go. But the woman said, 'Oh no, you mustn't! The night is black as pitch. I couldn't rest if I thought you were out wandering about in the dark at your age! You shall have my bed, if you will share it with the baby. I shall sleep soundly here in a chair by this lovely fire.'

So the wizard went to the woman's bed, and slept well enough. And the woman sat in a chair by the fire, and slept even better.

In the morning they ate what was left from supper; and again they had enough and to spare. Again the woman was astonished, and this time she did say something. She said, 'Sir, I think you cannot be what you seem; but whoever you are, I feel you have blessed us exceedingly.'

The wizard laughed. 'Yes,' he said, 'I have the power both to bless and to curse. I have also the power to make wishes come true. And so, for your kindness, I will grant you a wish. What shall it be?'

The woman remembered how she had planned that day to measure the piece of cloth her husband had left. Would it be a big piece, or would it be a small one? She did hope it would be a big piece! So she said, 'I would wish that the work I begin this morning may continue all day.'

'Your wish is granted,' said the wizard.

And when he had said that, he vanished in a puff of smoke.

The woman took the roll of cloth, opened it out on the table, and began to measure it. She measured a yard, two yards, three yards – and the more cloth she unrolled, the more there seemed to be left. When she had measured twelve yards, she took her scissors and cut off that length; but the roll that was left seemed even bigger now than it had been before. And what was more – the pattern of the cloth was changing. Whereas the first twelve yards had been useful dun-coloured homespun, the second twelve yards were richly coloured brocade; and when she had cut off this length,

the third twelve yards were shimmering silk; the fourth length
was of glowing velvet, the fifth of prettily patterned linen . . . and
so it went on. She unrolled and cut, unrolled and cut, and still
there was no end to the cloth, and still the material and the pattern
kept changing.

All day the woman unrolled and cut, till the cloth was piled up
to the rafters; the children were huddled together in the tiny bedroom. The neighbours came and tried to look in at the window,
but the window was blocked with the cloth; they peered over each
others' shoulders to look in at the door, but the cloth filled up the
doorway also, and the door would not open more than a few
inches.

Only at midnight did the widow come to the last twelve yards
of the cloth; and by that time she had enough cloth to stock five
towns, and of such innumerable designs and textures that there
was nothing that anyone could want in the way of material but
she could supply it.

So she rolled up the last twelve yards, blessed the lame beggar,
and went to her bed.

As you can guess, the poor widow's good fortune was talked
about everywhere, and the rich woman heard of it.

'Well, only fancy!' said the rich woman to her husband, 'what a
fool I have been! I could kick myself! But how was I to know that
the ugly lame beggar was a powerful wizard? If he comes this way
again, I shall behave very differently, I promise you!'

The wizard did come that way again. He came, as before, in the
guise of a lame beggar. And when he knocked at the rich woman's
door, she rushed to open it and bring him in.

'You poor dear old man!' she said. 'You must be tired and
hungry! You must rest and eat, you are welcome to all I possess!
For we are told, are we not, that those who relieve the needy shall
be blessed?'

She brought him into her best parlour; she bade the servants set meat and drink before him, she had a bath made ready for him, and brought out her husband's Sunday suit.

'Take this and put it on,' she said. 'If there were a better suit in the house, you should have it!'

But the wizard said he preferred to keep his rags, being accustomed to them.

So when he had eaten his fill, and washed himself and rested, he got up to go.

'But you must stay the night!' said the rich woman. 'I have the softest of soft beds ready for you. Come and see!'

She would have taken him into her best bedroom, where the servants had been busy cleaning and polishing, and lighting a fire in the hearth, and making up a bed with three feather mattresses, and silk sheets, down pillows, soft blankets and an embroidered quilt. But the wizard said no, he would go on his way, as it was yet early in the day, and he hoped to reach his own little cabin before nightfall.

'Madam,' said he, 'a poor old man, such as I am, has really nothing to offer you in return for your hospitality – except, of course, my thanks.'

'Nothing but your thanks!' cried the rich woman, growing all in a moment scowling and angry. 'A body can do well without anybody's thanks, I do think!'

'Well,' said the wizard, 'I can perhaps offer you something else. I can offer you a wish.'

Ah, that was better! The rich woman was all smiles again. 'I would wish,' she said, 'that the first work I do tomorrow at sunrise shall continue all day.'

'Your wish is granted,' said the wizard – and vanished in a puff of smoke.

The rich woman ran to her husband. 'I shall be more cunning than that foolish widow,' she said. 'Tomorrow at dawn I shall take out my purse and begin counting money; and so – just think of it! – I shall count money the whole of the day! Now I am going to cut out bags to put the money in.'

So she began cutting out bags. She cut them in round shapes, so that they need not be sewn, but just tied up with string. She began with any old scraps of material she could find; and when she had cut up all that, she looked round for something else.

'We shan't miss the old sheets,' she said.

So she cut up the old sheets.

The room soon became littered with cut-out bags. But still she said there weren't enough of them to hold all the money she would be counting next day. She cut up towels, she cut up pillow-cases, she cut up tablecloths. It grew late.

'Come to bed,' said her husband.

But no, she wouldn't.

'I am going to sit up all night, making bags,' she said. 'We can't have too many for all the money I shall be getting tomorrow.'

The husband went to bed. The woman ran into the best bedroom, dragged the sheets and blankets off the bed, and began cutting them up. And that room, too, was soon littered with cut-out bags.

Midnight struck. 'I have still many hours before dawn,' she thought. And she ran to open the wardrobe. There was her husband's best suit hanging up. 'Well, with the money I get tomorrow I can buy him all the good clothes in the world,' she said. And she snatched down that best suit from the wardrobe, and cut it up.

Cut, cut, cut: now it was her own dresses and petticoats – and still she wasn't satisfied. Cut, cut, cut – she dragged open every drawer in the house. Cut, cut, cut, at shirts and shifts and vests and pants. Cut, cut, cut, all through the night.

'Here is my Sunday bonnet,' she said, 'that will make capital strings to tie up the bags.'

Cut, cut, cut – the bonnet was in ribbons.

It was getting light now. Dawn reddened in the sky. The woman glanced out of the window. 'I shall begin counting money when the sun rises,' she said to herself, 'but I must just have two or three more bags.'

Cut, cut, cut – she slipped off the dress she was wearing and began cutting it up. She cut out one bag, she cut out two bags: she was just beginning on a third when the sun rose. There she was, standing in her petticoat, with the scissors in her hand, and the tail of her dress spread out on the floor. The bright beams of the rising sun glittered on the scissors – and the scissors stuck to her hand. She tried to put those scissors down to get out her purse and begin counting her money, but she couldn't.

Nor could she stop her hand from cutting out another bag from the tail of her dress. Nor, when that bag was cut out, could she stop cutting. She pulled down the curtains from the windows and cut them up; she dragged up the carpets from the floors, and began on them. Her hand was aching and her fingers were sore, but she could not stop.

Her husband came down: she rushed at him and began cutting the clothes off his back.

'Stop, stop, stop, are you mad?' he shouted.

'I can't stop,' she cried. 'Take the scissors from me, take them!'

He tried to wrench the scissors out of her grasp, but he could not. She cut away at his clothes till he had nothing on but his shirt, and then he ran from her howling. The servants came in: she cut their aprons, she cut their caps, she cut their print dresses. And they ran shrieking out of the house.

She was sobbing and shrieking herself now; but she could neither drop the scissors, nor stop cutting out bags. What she had been doing at sunrise she would continue to do all day – such had been her wish, and her wish had been granted.

Her husband had fled upstairs to his bed again. She followed him up. He drew the clothes up round his chin, and peeped at her from over the sheet.

'Go away!' he shouted.

But she dragged the bedclothes off him and cut them up; and he fled in his shirt out into the garden.

She was alone in the house, and the house was a wreck. She was howling with terror and disappointment, but still she couldn't stop cutting. She ran from room to room, and every room was a shambles, with empty drawers, and cupboards gaping wide, and the floors littered with cut-out bags.

Evening came, and still she was cutting. Midnight drew near, still she was cutting. She had nothing on but her chemise; she had cut up all her clothes, and even her chemise was getting shorter and shorter.

At five minutes to midnight came a puff of smoke: and there was the wizard standing at her side. He was wearing a flame-coloured robe, and he was carrying the beggar's cloak on his arm.

'Good evening,' said the wizard. 'I hope you have enjoyed your day?'

'Go away, you wicked, wicked man!' screamed the woman. 'Can't you see that in another moment I shall be naked?'

The wizard laughed. He took the beggar's cloak from his arm and flung it over her. She seized the edge of the cloak to cut it, but just then midnight struck, the scissors dropped from her hand, and huddled in the beggar's cloak she went to lie down in the remains of her bed.

Her husband came in. 'You have ruined us!' he shouted.

Well, if they weren't quite ruined, it cost them a pretty penny to put right all the havoc the rich woman had caused by her greed. The husband railed at his wife, the wife shouted back at her husband – and altogether they lived miserably.

As for the poor woman: with the money she got from the sale of the wonderful cloth she was able to keep her children and herself in comfort. And so they lived happily ever after.

II · *Cannetella*

Once upon a time there was a proud princess: Cannetella was her name. When she was eighteen years old, the king, her father, called her to him and said, 'My dear little daughter, we must find a husband for you.'

But Cannetella tossed up her lovely head, and said, 'I will not marry unless you find me a husband who is handsomer and cleverer and more charming than anyone else in the world.'

'We will do our best,' said the king. And he prepared a banquet, and sent out invitations to every handsome and clever and interesting young man he could hear of.

Well, well, when these handsome young men arrived, they were such a gallant company that the king said, 'Surely my dear little daughter, you can please yourself with one of these!'

But Cannetella frowned and pouted her lovely lips. 'None of them pleases me,' she said. And she found some fault with every one of them.

The king sent out more invitations, and held another banquet, and another company of gallant and handsome youths arrived. But Cannetella yawned and turned her back on them.

'Not one of them is good enough to be my lackey,' she said, 'much less to be my husband.'

The king tried a third time: the same thing – all no good. Then he was angry and said, 'I see how it is with you, my girl; you do not intend to marry at all! But marry someone you must and shall, for you are my heir.'

'Oh, very well, Papa,' said the naughty Cannetella. 'If you can find me a man with a gold head and teeth of gold, I give you my word – I will marry him.'

So the king sent out a proclamation to say that any man with a gold head and gold teeth might come forward and marry his daughter; and he would throw in the kingdom as a wedding gift, for he felt like going into a monastery, so greatly had Cannetella vexed him.

Now there was a wizard called Sciorovante; and when he heard the proclamation, Sciorovante skipped for joy. He drew a great many magic circles, and muttered a great many magic words, and seven little imps came hopping along, all calling out, 'What is your will, master? What is your will?'

Sciorovante bade them make him a golden head immediately; and the imps ran off and set to work. Very soon they were back with the golden head. Sciorovante fitted it on, and grinned at himself in a looking-glass. The head gleamed, and the gold teeth glittered: it was frightful to look on. But Sciorovante was well pleased, and gave the imps a week's holiday.

Then he went to ride on his black horse up and down outside the palace.

The king looked out of a window and said, 'Hullo! Hullo! Here is the very man we are looking for!' And he sent a servant to summon Sciorovante to come to him.

When Sciorovante came in, the king said, 'My good sir, I don't know who you are or where you come from, nor do I much care. But my daughter has chosen you for her husband.'

And he sent for Cannetella.

Cannetella was in her room, trying on some new dresses. When she heard the king wanted her, she said, 'Oh bother!' and did not go. The king sent for her three times; and at last Cannetella went to him, wearing one of her new dresses, and flaunting along with her nose in the air.

By this time the king was fuming. 'I have found you the husband you asked for,' he said. 'Here he is! And I hope you may live long and happily with him!'

Cannetella nearly fainted. For Sciorovante was a huge man, and his golden nose was long and hooked, and his golden eyes were deep set and gleaming; his golden lips leered, and his golden teeth grinned and glittered. But Cannetella was too proud to show how much afraid she was.

'We will hold the wedding at once,' said the king. 'I'm not giving you time to go back on your word!'

Cannatella tossed up her lovely head. 'I do not intend to go back on my word,' she said.

The king was bustling off to give orders for the wedding, when Sciorovante said, 'If I am to wed your daughter, I prefer to wed her in my own country.'

'Oh very well, very well,' said the king. 'Do as you please! Take her away and marry her. And when you want my kingdom – come back and claim it!'

So Sciorovante set Cannetella up before him on his black horse and galloped away.

The black horse outstripped the wind; the earth flew backward under his hoofs. All day he was galloping.

In the evening, they came to a stable, and the black horse stopped with such a jerk that Cannetella was flung from his back on to the road. Sciorovante swung himself out of the saddle and pulled Cannetella to her feet. With one hand he led the horse, with the other hand he led Cannetella, and he took them both into the stable. There were seven stalls in the stable; in every stall but one stood a white horse, but the seventh stall was empty. Sciorovante led the black horse and Cannetella into the empty stall.

'Now,' said he, 'listen to me. I am going to my home to arrange for our wedding, and my home is seven years' journey from here. You must wait for me in this stable, and never move out of it, or let yourself be seen by a living soul. If you obey me, well and good. If you disobey me – woe betide you!'

Cannetella's proud spirit had died within her. She said, 'I am your servant and must do as you bid me. But I beg you to tell me what I am going to live on till you return.'

'You can take what the horses leave,' said Sciorovante.

He went away, and Cannetella sat down in the straw at the feet of the black horse and wept.

'Oh what a bad, silly girl I have been!' she cried. It was all her own fault, and she knew it; but that didn't make her feel any happier.

She had no one to comfort her, not even the horses. They shrugged away from her when she tried to stroke them, for Sciorovante had hardened their hearts. Every morning and every evening they were fed and watered by invisible hands; and Cannetella had to quench her thirst out of their water buckets, and stay her hunger with what was left of their bran and oats. In this manner she lived for many months, growing all the time thinner and paler and more miserable.

One morning, when she was pacing up and down the stable, wringing her hands, she noticed a little crack in the wall. She looked through this crack and saw a beautiful garden: there were vines heavy with grapes, and trees laden down with apples and plums and oranges. The sight was more than Cannetella could bear.

'I must and will have some of that fruit!' she said to herself. 'I will slip out and pick some. Sciorovante is far away – who is to tell him what I do? And even should he find out, he cannot make my life more miserable than it is now.'

The stable door wasn't locked. Cannetella lifted the latch, opened the door and stepped into the garden. She plucked the fruit and ate till she could eat no more, for she was half-starved. Then she went back into the stable, taking with her some plums and oranges to eat next day.

And next day, when she had eaten the plums and oranges, she wrapped the stones and the peel in her handkerchief, meaning to take it all out and bury it in the garden. She lifted the latch to open the stable door, but the door would not open. She pulled and rattled at that door till her arms ached – all no good, it would not open. So she put the peel and the plum stones into the black horse's manger, and covered them over with hay.

That evening, to her dismay, Sciorovante came back. He didn't look at Cannetella. He went up to the black horse, pulled its ears and said, 'Well, my horse, and how have things gone on here?'

'Look under the hay in my manger,' said the black horse.

Sciorovante looked under the hay: there were the plum stones and the orange peel. He turned on Cannetella in a fury.

'Didn't I tell you not to move from the stable?' he yelled. 'Didn't I say woe betide you if you disobeyed? Now I am going to kill you!'

And he took a huge knife from his girdle.

But Cannetella knelt and flung her arms about his knees, and begged him to spare her life. She said she had been hungry – oh so hungry! That indeed she would have died if she had not eaten the fruit.

She wept and implored until at last Sciorovante put away his knife and said, 'Well, I will forgive you this time. But if you disobey me again, if when I return I hear that you have so much as moved out of the stall, I *will* kill you! Now I am going away again, and I shall be absent for seven years.'

How Cannetella hated the black horse! Though it was not his fault, poor beast – Sciorovante had him under a spell. But Cannetella dared not go into the garden again, and for a whole year she lived on oats and bran. Then one day she heard the patter of hoofs and the sound of wheels outside the stable. And she heard another sound too: someone was whistling a tune she knew. Someone, then, from her own country! She ran to the stable door, hammered on it and called, 'Save me! Save me! Open the door, it is not locked, but I dare not come out!'

The door was pushed open, and a round astonished face looked in. It was the king's cooper, who made his wine barrels for him.

'Who are you?' said the cooper. 'And what are you doing here?'

'Am I so changed that you don't recognize me?' cried Cannetella. 'I am the Princess Cannetella, your king's daughter.'

And she began to sob and told the cooper the whole of her story.

'I have an empty barrel in my cart,' said the cooper. 'Come, I will hide you in it, and take you home.'

So Cannetella got into the barrel, and the cooper got up on the front of the cart, and urged his mule on at its utmost speed. The mule was big and sturdy, but it took them a long, long time to reach the king's palace. And when they got there at last, it was the middle of the night. The palace was in darkness, and everyone was asleep.

The cooper knocked on the door with all his might. The servants woke and came running in a hurry. But when they saw the cooper with the cart, they were indignant.

'What an hour to deliver a barrel! Go away, and come back in the morning!'

The servants would have shut the door again, but the cooper kept it open with his foot.

'Wake the king and bring him here,' he said. 'I have something of importance to deliver.'

So they fetched the king, and he came, not at all pleased, rubbing his eyes and yawning. 'What is it *now*?' he said.

'I would crave your patience whilst I unload my cart,' said the cooper. 'And if your patience is not rewarded, you may cut off my head.'

'Well, well, unload it then!' said the king. And he bade a servant help the cooper to lift down the barrel.

And when the barrel was on the ground, the cooper took off the lid, and Cannetella crawled out.

The king gave a shriek. 'My little daughter, my princess, my Cannetella – is it possible?'

'Yes, Papa,' said Cannetella, 'it is your poor unhappy little daughter.'

The king kissed her again and again and again. He brought her into the palace; he plied her with meat and drink; he had all the ladies-in-waiting running to fetch clothes for her – for she was in rags. He had long ago repented of having let the gold-headed man carry her off, he had long ago forgotten all her spoilt ways. And as Cannetella had long ago repented of those spoilt ways, they wept in each other's arms, and comforted each other.

But in the meantime, Sciorovante had returned to the stable. And when he saw that Cannetella had gone, he screamed out, 'My horse, my horse, where is the princess?'

And the black horse answered, 'The king's cooper came and took her away in a barrel.'

When Sciorovante heard that, he ran the black horse out of the stable, leaped on his back, and galloped off to the king's city.

There he called his imps, bade them take off his gold head and return his own head to him. And when this was done, he took lodgings with an old woman who lived opposite the palace.

He said to the old woman, 'I will give you a hundred ducats if you will let me go up on to your roof that I may catch a glimpse of the king's daughter.'

The old woman was delighted to let him go up on her roof for a hundred ducats – she would have let him go up for much less. So Sciorovante looked across at the palace, and what did he see? He saw Cannetella sitting at a window combing her long hair.

Cannetella looked out of the window, and what did *she* see? She saw Sciorovante glaring at her from the roof top. His gold head

was gone, but she knew him! She flung down the comb and rushed to the king.

'Papa! Papa! He has come! Sciorovante has come! Unless you lock me up in a room with seven iron doors I am lost for ever!'

The king called for his locksmiths; the iron doors were quickly made, and Cannetella was securely shut in behind them. But Sciorovante summoned his imps, and they told him what the king had done. Then Sciorovante went to the old woman and showed her a rose-coloured bowl.

'This is a rare piece,' he said. 'I had it from a Chinaman. I will give you five hundred ducats if you will take it as a present to the princess. Put it into her hands, and whilst she is admiring it, slip this paper under her pillow. Oh, it is nothing – just a little loving message from an admirer.'

The old woman was full of glee at the thought of earning the five hundred ducats so easily. She couldn't read, and so she didn't know what was written on the paper. It was this: *May all other folk be fast asleep, and only Cannetella be left awake.*

Off went the old woman with the bowl and the slip of paper. The bowl was very beautiful. When the king saw it, he thought: 'This will please my little daughter.' So he had the old woman taken into the room behind the seven iron doors. And whilst Cannetella was admiring the bowl and wondering who could have sent her such a pretty present, the old woman slipped the piece of paper under her pillow.

Immediately all the people in the palace, including the old woman, fell into a heavy sleep: only Cannetella was left awake.

Sciorovante hurried to the palace. Cannetella heard a thunderous banging on the iron doors. She screamed with terror, but no one heard her: everyone in the palace lay as if dead. *Bang! Bang! Bang!* The iron doors shook and rattled. Cannetella went on screaming; one after another the iron doors buckled and bowed and fell down, and Sciorovante rushed in.

Cannetella ran to the farthest corner of the room. She jumped on to the bed and clung to it, all huddled up; she was still screaming. Sciorovante picked her up, bed and all. He was striding out of the room with her when he stumbled over one of the smashed-in iron doors; he gave a jerk to recover his balance – and the piece of paper fell out from under the pillow and fluttered to the floor.

In an instant everyone in the palace woke up. They heard Cannetella's screams and rushed to the rescue. King and courtiers, lords-in-waiting and ladies-in-waiting, cooks, scullions, grooms, and stable boys, even the dogs and cats – with swords and cudgels, with knives and scissors, with ladles and rolling pins, with horse whips and halters, with teeth and claws, one and all fell upon Sciorovante.

Sciorovante turned himself into a lion and roared – swords slashed him; he turned himself into a serpent and hissed – knives stabbed him; he turned himself into a fire and blazed – buckets of water doused him; he turned himself into a hare – the dogs harried him; he turned himself into a rat – the cats pounced on him; he turned himself into a gnat, and was just about to escape up the chimney, when the king spied him. The king clapped his hands together, caught the gnat between his hands and squashed it – and that was the end of Sciorovante.

And by and by a prince came wooing Cannetella. The prince was neither handsomer nor cleverer nor more charming than many another prince; but when the king said to Cannetella, 'Will you have him?' Cannetella curtsied to the ground, and said, 'If you please, Papa.'

So the king was made happy, and the prince was made happy, and Cannetella was happy also. And they all lived merrily ever after.

And if you want to know what happened to the black horse: well, he was free now; so he galloped back to the stable and kicked it down. Then he and the six white horses trotted off to their native pastures – and they too lived merrily ever after.